# BETRAYED IN THE WILD

## RYAN CUDDY

C&F ALPINE PUBLISHING

Publisher Details: C&F Alpine Publishing
ISBN: 979-8-9904992-0-1

This book is a work of fiction. Names, characters, places, and incidents are the product of the author's imagination or are used fictitiously. Any resemblance to actual events, locales, or persons, living or dead, is coincidental.

Visit Ryan-Cuddy.com for more information about the author and upcoming releases.

The journey of creating this book has been far from linear. Over the past four years, amid the whirlwind of life events—marriage, home purchases, and the joyous chaos of welcoming two children—I've found solace and inspiration in the process, even during the weeks or months when the book sat on the back burner.

I extend my deepest gratitude to my wife, whose constant support and understanding enabled me to embark on this literary journey. Her encouragement and patience during these chaotic years have been my anchor.

A special thank you to my parents and in-laws for their alpha-reading efforts, which provided invaluable insights and critiques that refined the early stages of *Betrayed in the Wild.*

Appreciation is also extended to the beta readers who dedicated their time and gave constructive feedback during the late phase of the manuscript. Your input has been crucial in finalizing the narrative.

I am immensely grateful to my editors for their invaluable guidance and expertise. Thank you for helping me refine and shape this novel into its final form.

Ryan Cuddy

This book is dedicated to the memory of my dear sister, Jami Cuddy. Her unwavering confidence, brilliant intellect, and fierce determination served as guiding inspirations for the qualities I hoped to capture in Olivia's character. She is in my thoughts daily, and I hope I have portrayed this character to reflect even a fraction of your remarkable example.

In loving memory of Jami Cuddy—forever a source of inspiration.

# 1

"Leave the talking to me, Owen. I don't want you to say anything that could set these guys off. Actually, just stay in the plane," Terry said as the landing gear of his small passenger plane touched down on a remote Alaskan tarmac.

The aircraft taxied around the runway until its lights illuminated a metal hangar, the only structure in sight. It crawled through the large open door, and the plane's engines groaned to a halt. Before Terry opened his door, a black SUV pulled in behind. Three men exited the vehicle and sealed the hangar door, isolating them from the outside world.

The headlights momentarily blinded Terry as he fumbled for the door handle. He finally grasped the frigid metal lever and opened the door. Shielding his eyes with his hand, he made his way toward the rear of the plane. Once there, he found one of the men from the vehicle struggling with the plane's back hatch.

"I got it." Terry nudged the man out of the way. "You have to pull up and then right at the same time to open it," he explained, swinging the door open with a loud creak that echoed throughout the hangar. "Needs WD-40," he added, trying to elicit a reaction from the man.

The man didn't acknowledge him as he retrieved a bulging cardboard box from the plane and disappeared into the shadows behind the vehicle. Another man approached, and Terry assumed he was the driver. He wore a black leather jacket, dark denim jeans, and a pair of cowboy boots that had never seen a saddle, let alone a prairie. Terry's eyes focused on the black duffle bag in the man's hand just as he placed it down beside him.

"Is this all of it?" Terry inquired.

"Every dollar," confirmed the driver.

Terry unzipped the bag, revealing stacks of cash, and said, "You don't mind if I take a look, do you?"

The man remained silent. Instead, he glared deep into Terry's eyes.

"You know what? It looks like everything's here," Terry said, changing his mind and zipping the bag back up.

"Mind if I double-check?" asked Owen, appearing from the shadows.

"I do mind. It's there," Terry snapped, wrestling the bag into the plane's cargo hold.

The driver nodded before he walked back to his vehicle. Meanwhile, the other two men rolled open the large metal hangar door. They all loaded up into their vehicle before it backed up and drove away, vanishing into a cloak of darkness.

The two pilots stood watching until the vehicle was no longer visible. Terry retrieved a small flashlight from his jacket pocket and turned it on. He shined it at his plane before gesturing for Owen to close the back hatch while he boarded the weathered plane.

"What did I tell you about talking?" Terry scolded when Owen entered the cockpit.

Owen set his jaw but lowered his eyes and said, "I'm sorry, it won't happen again."

"It better not," Terry muttered as he ignited the plane's engine. It groaned and moaned and grinded before finally turning over. He gently patted the old bird, then shifted it into gear and maneuvered it out of the hangar.

# 2

The porch boards creaked under Olivia's feet as she stepped outside and embraced the crisp Alaskan morning. Steam swirled from the floral mug she held, filling the air with the rich aroma of coffee.

She took a slow sip and let the heat seep deep into her bones. The vintage mug had been a gift from her grandma during a visit two years prior. Fond memories came flooding back as she took in the breathtaking vista of the mountains, transporting her back to a cherished moment spent with her grandma.

***

The morning sunlight had pierced into the room, but her body pleaded for more sleep. Olivia had driven from Bozeman to Red Lodge late last night after she had longed for the comfort of her grandma's company.

The metal-framed bed and Grandma's quilt wrapped her soul in familiar comfort, and it wasn't until the ding of a kitchen timer, followed by a tempting aroma wafting from the kitchen, lured her out of bed. The sweet fusion of cranberries and oranges permeated the air. Grandma was baking her favorite muffins, and they were almost done.

She quietly opened the creaking door, making her way down the hallway. She patiently watched as her grandma opened the oven door, pulled out a fresh pan of muffins, and rested them on the counter.

"Good morning, Grandma. Those smell amazing. How did you know this was exactly what I needed?" Olivia said.

"Livvy." Her grandma smiled and embraced her in a warm hug. "I take it your drive was good?"

"Long but uneventful."

"I got you a present. Go have a seat, and I'll bring it over with a muffin," she replied, gently shooing her out of the kitchen.

Olivia settled in the living room and sunk into the oversized, black leather recliner next to the fireplace—the same recliner where she and her grandma used to read books on the nights she visited as a child.

"Livvy, dear, how are you holding up?" Grandma asked as she returned bearing her gift: a floral mug filled with hot coffee and a warm cranberry orange muffin.

Olivia sighed, her shoulders slumped. "Not well, Grandma. It's been a really tough couple of months since…" She paused, a tear beginning to fall down her cheek. She wiped it away. "I only have a few more weeks until I'm done with college, and all my energy has gone toward that."

Grandma reached over and squeezed her hand. "I'm so sorry, Livvy. Have you put any thought into what you want to do after?"

"None."

"I have an idea. Let me make a couple of phone calls."

The two had spent hours by the fire that morning, grieving and telling stories about the past, while also wondering what the future held.

***

She hadn't seen her grandma since she arrived in Alaska, but they still spoke on the phone weekly. Glancing at her watch, she smiled. Their next call was only two days away.

The distant peaks sparkled under a fresh blanket of snow. Olivia knew the fishing season would be ending soon, but that didn't mean her job as a fishing guide was over yet. In fact, there was at least another month of guest reservations ahead. While she would have loved nothing more than to savor her coffee and continue to lose herself in the awe-inspiring scenery, the day was packed.

She enjoyed one last sip before retreating to her cabin to finish getting ready. With practiced grace, she moved through her one-room bungalow toward the wardrobe. She put on a blue-and-white checkered fishing shirt and gray quick-dry pants, then grabbed her waders that were sprawled across the shower curtain rod. They were still damp from the previous day, but that made them easier to slip on. Although, she could do without the pungent, musky odor mixed with fish slime. Before heading out the door, she grabbed her favorite blue ball cap, sunglasses, and fishing bag.

Her boots crunched over gravel as she made her way down the short trail to the main cabin. This was where most of the guests stayed, except for two spacious log cabins nestled on the riverside. Naturally, those were the most coveted accommodations on the property.

She gripped the cold steel handle of the main cabin's large wooden door and forced it open before walking down the main corridor, past the numerous framed pictures of guests posing with salmon, grizzly bears, and majestic mountain lakes. As she entered the dining hall, the buzz of guests conversing and silverware clanking against plates filled the air. She headed toward the buffet, grabbed a plate, and helped herself to two fried eggs, three slices of bacon, and a mixed fruit and yogurt parfait. As she poured a second cup of coffee, a familiar voice rang out before she could look around for a place to sit.

"Olivia, come join us," invited a tall, lanky man with his wife seated by his side. They were her clients for the day and had become acquainted the night before over a bourbon. They mostly talked about the couple's growing business, but she also learned they were experienced and enthusiastic anglers. She enjoyed teaching clients how to fly fish but was always relieved when she knew she could concentrate more on fishing than untangling knots.

"Morning, Malcolm. Hi, Zoey," Olivia greeted with a warm smile, setting her plate next to them. "How'd you sleep?"

"Terrible, not a wink. I was too excited for the day," Malcolm responded.

"Not a wink, huh?" Zoey interjected. "You kept me up all night snoring!"

Olivia grinned. Today would be entertaining if this continued.

Over breakfast, the three continued their conversation from the night prior, and Olivia detailed her expectations for the day. She intended to take them down the main channel by boat before they would wade up a small tributary and spend the day fishing for rainbow trout, grayling, and the occasional arctic char. However, they were in grizzly country, so she ensured they were aware of the risks and comfortable with bear spray.

"Have you ever actually seen a grizzly?" Malcolm asked. "A fishing guide back in Yellowstone spun us the same tale, but we never saw one. I'm starting to doubt they're real."

Olivia chuckled. "Oh, I've had my fair share of grizzly encounters. They can be quite intimidating. And I've fished in Yellowstone more than a few times, running into some bears there myself. Luckily, it was never an issue, but bear spray might save your life if we cross paths with one today."

Malcolm beamed, but Zoey nodded in acknowledgment, her face tight as she set her napkin on her plate. With that, the couple excused themselves to their room to collect their fishing gear before reconvening at the boat.

Olivia finished her breakfast and walked through the swinging door labeled "Staff Only" toward the back of the kitchen. She opened a giant refrigerator door and retrieved three sack lunches the kitchen staff had prepared. Peeking inside each brown bag, saw the familiar contents: a turkey and cheese sandwich, condiments, an apple, a bag of chips, and a homemade chocolate chip cookie. Her favorite. As she folded the bags closed, she jumped, startled by the sudden appearance of Felix beside her.

"Come on, Olivia. You're not really that jumpy, are you?" asked Felix, one of the other fishing guides at the lodge.

Olivia laughed to hide her embarrassment. "I guess I am. Who are you guiding today? Where are you headed to?"

"I have Henry for the day. He mentioned you took him up north and floated yesterday, so we are going to float downstream and check out that large pool on the side channel," he said.

Olivia stared at him in bewilderment. "You mean the one with the momma grizzly bear you spotted last week? You know, the one that bluff charged you?"

Felix's face turned bright red. "Yeah, that's the place. There's no way she's still there, Olivia. It's been a week, and the fishing there is incredible. I can't pass that up."

"Well, good luck. Hopefully, she's moved on by now, but make sure you have a fresh can of bear spray or two. Henry is one of the good ones. I would hate to see him become bear food. You, on the other hand, it seems inevitable."

Felix smirked and leaned against the refrigerator door. "Yeah, I deserve that. Tell me more about Henry. I haven't gotten a chance to talk to him yet."

"Sure. He's some sort of college professor back east—New Hampshire, Vermont, or Connecticut—one of those states. Anyway, he's a genuine family man. He's been on a fishing trip like this every year for the last fifteen years, so he's a seasoned angler. He mentioned he started going on trips with his son, but we didn't get too much into it. It seemed like a sore subject to me."

"Seasoned angler? That's what I like to hear. Less teaching and more fishing. Do you think he'd mind if I fished a little too?" Felix said with a mischievous grin across his face.

"If only that were acceptable. I haven't caught a fish since my last day off here. That had to have been sometime early last season."

"Brian gave you a day off? Incredible," Felix said before he gestured to his watch. "Looks like it's time to head down to the boat. Have a wonderful day with the Mr. and Mrs." He snagged two of the three lunches out of Olivia's hand with a wink and walked out of the kitchen.

"Watch out for that momma bear, Felix!" Olivia shouted as the door slammed shut.

She reached into the refrigerator once more and replaced her stolen lunches before finding her way back outside. As she descended the gravel pathway toward the docks, she passed Felix heading back up to the lodge. "Don't worry, Olivia. I'll get your gas," he sarcastically said as he hauled two empty red gas cans.

"The least you can do," she countered as she walked past him, holding up her replaced lunch bags.

The docks were an eyesore spot in the lodge's luxurious appearance. Guests occasionally tripped over warped cedar boards long overdue for a fresh coat of sealant. The weathered docks also only housed two boats, limiting the number of guides and, thus, fishing opportunities at the lodge.

Olivia felt a sense of pride as she reached her twenty-foot skiff with a forty-horsepower engine. This was her boat, or rather, she was the only guide to take it out. Brian, the general manager, had purchased the boat during her first season. Despite Felix's seniority, he'd chosen to stick with his original boat, citing an attachment to it. Olivia respected his choice and didn't press the matter, secretly pleased that it meant the new boat belonged exclusively to her. She hopped over the side of the boat and opened the hard-sided cooler stocked with water bottles, ice, and beer—something she had done the night before to ensure she got an extra five minutes of sleep this morning.

She tossed in the three lunches before she placed her fishing bag down. Reaching into a large metal tube attached to the side of the boat, she pulled out a fly rod. It still had the streamer that Henry used yesterday attached. She removed it and picked up her fly box from her pack. Putting the streamer away, she reviewed all the options and settled on a black stonefly trailed by a pink egg pattern.

As she finished tying the new flies on, Felix returned to the dock. He glanced at what she had tied on and scoffed in a disgusted tone. "An egg pattern? Really, Olivia? Have some respect, would you?"

"Listen, this is why our clients prefer me. I use flies that catch fish rather than worrying about what people on Instagram think."

Felix smirked and set a can of gas down in her boat before he headed over to his boat.

"Thanks, Felix," Olivia said as she secured it toward the back. She finished setting up the other rod to match when Malcolm and Zoey made their way down.

"I can't get over how beautiful this place is," Zoey said as she stepped onto the dock.

"Out of this world," Malcolm agreed.

Olivia took a moment to absorb the surroundings, viewing the fishing lodge through her guests' eyes. This place had been her sanctuary for the past two fishing seasons, a refuge from her former life. The lodge sat nestled along the shores of the Naknek River—a large, slow-moving river teeming with trout, arctic grayling, arctic char, and every type of salmon imaginable—which granted access to numerous tributaries. It offered an extraordinary small-river fishing experience to its clientele. All these wild waterways were framed by the rugged yet captivating peaks in the distance.

"It really is a beautiful place," Olivia said, snapping out of her thoughts. "Have you ever been to Alaska before?"

"First time. We're no strangers to fishing in the West though. We've been to Colorado and Montana a few times. Yellowstone, too, of course. That was pretty, but nothing compared to this," Zoey replied as she continued to take in the vista.

"I grew up in Montana, just outside of Red Lodge. It's a great place, but this is something special," Olivia said.

A short man wearing a Vermont ball cap and flannel shirt stepped onto the dock. His sunglasses and dark beard concealed most of his face, but Olivia recognized him from yesterday.

"Hi, Henry," she greeted.

"Hello, Olivia. Looks like they switched up the guides on me."

"They sure did. We had an amazing outing yesterday, didn't we? Felix is pretty good too, and I think we're matched again tomorrow, if I'm not mistaken."

"We sure are. Tomorrow's my last day, so think of somewhere special, yeah?"

Olivia nodded, and Henry walked by Zoey and Malcolm to shake hands with Felix.

"Stay safe, you two," she said to Henry and Felix before redirecting her full attention to her guests. "Let's get loaded and on the river." She extended a hand to help them onto the boat.

Once the guests settled on the leather bucket seats at the bow of the boat, Olivia turned the key and the engine roared to life. She untied the ropes, adjusted the throttle, and turned the boat upriver.

# 3

As Olivia navigated the boat upriver, she noticed the couple pointing out various rapids and the surrounding mountains. Malcolm turned back to her, his hands waving and signaling for her to stop. She pulled back on the throttle and maneuvered out of the main channel as Malcolm pointed across the river, whispering, "Moose!" He reached into his bag and took out a camera, attaching a large telephoto lens to it. Although Olivia had seen dozens of moose throughout the season, she was still as mesmerized as the first time she saw one. This one was massive, and its giant antlers glistened in the morning sun.

Malcolm's camera clicked incessantly as he captured shot after shot of the wild animal. He turned to Olivia, his face featuring a broad grin. "This is the first time I've seen one in the wild," he exclaimed before eagerly resuming his photographic frenzy.

Olivia blinked, remembering the last time she heard a camera clicking furiously at a moose.

***

It was freshman year in college, and she found herself with a cute boy named James, whom she had recently met in her General Biology class. They were floating on the Upper Madison River in Montana. It was a beautiful spring day during the Mother's Day Caddis hatch, with the sun shining down on them after a long, frigid winter. Olivia was more grateful for the warmth on her skin that day than any of the fish she caught. James sat in the back of the boat, idly trailing his fishing pole.

James was tall and lean, with disheveled brown hair that glimmered in the sun. His easy smile and relaxed demeanor added to his charm, making him effortlessly captivating. Despite his casual nature, there was a thoughtful glint in his eyes, hinting at a deeper intellect beneath his laid-back exterior. Olivia found herself drawn to his quiet confidence and genuine kindness, grateful for his presence on that beautiful spring day.

As they rounded a bend, she noticed movement coming from the brush on the shore. She brought the boat to a halt as a strong, musky odor overtook her. A gigantic moose emerged, giving out a deep bellow before gracefully splashing into the water. She couldn't contain her excitement as the moose began to swim across the river, its massive body cutting through the current.

James, giddy with excitement, put his fishing pole down and picked up his cell phone, taking photo after photo. Olivia watched in wonder, humbled by the sheer size and power of the creature. She was also struck by James's enthusiasm for the natural world and his willingness to let his emotions overwhelm him, which became one of her favorite qualities about him.

***

The moose lifted his long brown head and peered up at his onlookers, then wandered back into the foliage and disappeared.

"That was the coolest thing I've ever seen!" Malcolm said.

"Did you get a good shot?" Zoey asked as she leaned over to view the camera screen.

"Tons! Do you know that place in the living room where I've always said something is missing? This is what's missing." Malcolm showed her a photo from his camera.

Olivia couldn't help but smile as she watched the couple scrolling through the pictures, debating which photo was best. She pushed down on the throttle once more and continued upriver to her favorite tributary.

As Olivia approached the river's bank, she gradually reduced the engine speed to a halt. The water rippled against the boat's metal frame as it glided to shore. Moving toward the starboard side, she unwound the rope anchored aboard. Just as she had enough slack in hand, the boat contacted the shore, and she leaped off, securing the rope to a nearby stump.

"Wow, that was impressive," Zoey said, applauding.

"A pro move right there," added Malcolm.

Olivia's cheeks flushed with gratitude. "Thank you. I've had my fair share of experience with this," she responded before hopping back onto the boat with flawless ease.

She leaned in next to her guests and began her rehearsed spiel—one that she had shaped and refined into what it was today after a few hundred expeditions. "Before we start fishing, I need to review some important safety information. While this stream may be smaller than the Naknek River, it still has its own set of dangers."

Pausing for effect, she adjusted her hat and continued, "There are spots where the river is deceptively deep and has strong undertows. So please, only cross where I instruct and never leave my sight."

"Additionally, it's important to be aware of the wildlife in this area. While I know seeing moose and bears is exciting, they can be dangerous." Her hand instinctively went to her belt, where her bear spray was holstered. "So, make sure you always have your bear spray and know how to use it. Safety first."

As she finished, she straightened up and clapped her hands together. "Alright, let's catch some fish! We're all rigged up and ready to go, but if you happen to snag a log or break off, I'll get it replaced for you. Any questions?"

"Hey, do you mind doing us a favor?" Malcolm asked. "Would you carry my camera? We'd really love some action shots and, of course, the classic fish-in-hand pictures."

"Now, what kind of fishing guide would I be if I didn't know how to take a photo?" Olivia took the camera from Malcolm before handing both him and Zoey a fly rod.

As the two guests stepped off the boat and onto the grassy shore, Olivia grabbed her fishing bag and net and pointed to a large cottonwood tree up ahead.

The old tree stood tall and wide, its sizable yellowing canopy shading the stream. "Let's start up there. Yesterday, we pulled a huge char out of that pool, and I bet it's still there. Zoey, how about you take the first crack?"

"With pleasure!" Zoey beamed over at Malcolm. She strolled toward the tree while Olivia and Malcolm gave her space and settled in the sun to watch. Zoey unhooked the fly from its resting spot and let out some fly line. The neon-yellow line flowed back and forth as she cast with the ease of a seasoned angler. Olivia focused Malcolm's camera, capturing the moment just as Zoey placed the line directly upstream of a deep, slow-moving pool.

The white strike indicator disappeared underwater in an instant, and Zoey set the hook with a slight twitch of her wrist. Her reel instantly screeched as the fish darted upriver.

"Great job, Zoey!" Malcolm cheered while Olivia snapped more shots and offered words of encouragement.

"I think I've got a big one!" Zoey shouted when she gained control of her rod and started reeling in the fish. A few minutes of anticipation passed as she worked the fish. Olivia made her way down to her, holding her net firmly in hand. As the fish got close enough, Olivia scooped up the giant arctic char into the net. She then handed the handle over to Zoey.

"Congratulations, Zoey. That's a monster!" Olivia said.

Zoey's eyes sparkled with wonder as she admired the fish's striking red belly and the white highlighted fins. "Wow, it's stunning. This is my first char!"

"Hold it up, I'll take a picture," Olivia said, snapping some shots when Zoey proudly displayed her prized catch. Then, turning to Malcolm, Olivia urged, "Get in there with her! This one's frame-worthy." She continued to take a few more photos before it was time for Zoey to release the fish.

Zoey carefully removed the fly from the fish's mouth and eased it out of the net and into the water, facing its head toward the stream's current. She supported its belly until it recovered enough strength to kick away and slowly return to the depths of the pool. Zoey turned to Olivia. "Thank you. That was remarkable."

Olivia's eyes glistened with joy. The sun was warm on her skin, and the sound of the rushing river was music to her ears. Moments like this were why she had become a guide. It wasn't just about catching fish but about the memories. She loved being a part of that, of helping people create something special they could treasure forever.

Back home in Montana, things had been tough. Complicated. Painful. But out here on the river, it was different. It was a place of peace and beauty, where the pain of the world melted away. Guiding was her escape—her refuge from her past. Moments like this—witnessing the pure joy on Zoey's face—reminded her why she cherished this life so deeply.

The day continued with Zoey and Malcolm catching numerous rainbow trout, grayling, and a few smaller salmon. Malcolm even landed a smaller char, but nothing quite matched the thrill of that first fish.

As the trio walked back to the boat, Malcolm stopped and reached for Olivia's hand, discreetly slipping a wad of cash into it.

"Oh, Malcolm, you know I can't accept this," Olivia said gently, handing him the money back. "It's incredibly thoughtful of you, but accepting tips goes against the lodge's policy."

"I know, I know. I wasn't planning on doing this, but please take it. It's the least I can do to repay you. We've fished all over with dozens of guides, and you've been the best by far. Everyone always prioritizes me catching the biggest or the most fish, but you made sure today was about my wife." Malcolm held out the money with genuine appreciation in his eyes. "Please. Take it."

Zoey nodded in enthusiastic agreement. "Absolutely! You made this fishing trip unforgettable, and we want you to know how much we value your expertise and guidance."

Olivia hesitated for a moment, touched by their words and sincerity. "I really appreciate your kind words." After a brief pause, she hesitantly accepted the wad of cash and smiled warmly, tucking it into her wader pocket. "Thank you."

# 4

On the dock, Olivia was cleaning her boat and restocking the cooler with fresh ice and beverages when she noticed Brian approaching. Brian rarely made it down to the docks, so a wave of panic washed over her. *Did they tell him I took the tip?*

"Olivia, do you have a minute to talk?" He spoke in a more serious tone than usual and avoided making eye contact. Something was wrong.

She nodded and tried to maintain her composure. "I do. I'm just getting the boat ready for Henry tomorrow."

Brian paused before taking a deep breath. "I got a call from your dad this morning. I'll take care of all this and take Henry out tomorrow. Go up to my office and give him a call. The news should come from him."

He offered a small smile and placed a hand on her shoulder. "Come find me afterward, and we'll discuss what's next."

She felt her heart sink. Thoughts rushed through her mind as she tried to figure out why her father had called. *What news could he possibly have to cause Brian to act like this?* "Okay, Brian. I'll give him a call," she said, her voice quivering.

Olivia stumbled on a loose board when she stepped out of the boat. Brian grabbed her arm and steadied her. "Thanks, Brian," she managed to say.

With each step away from the docks, she felt the ground beneath her become more unstable. The gravel path winding toward the lodge stretched forever, as if time itself had slowed down. Her heart thundered in her chest, but the noise of her boots on the gravel was even louder. *Was it about Mom? Is it his job? Was there an accident?*

She arrived at the lodge and trudged down a dimly lit side corridor. Her hand trembled when she reached for the door labeled "Management." Pushing it open, Olivia entered the cluttered office. Torn envelopes and candy wrappers were scattered in piles over the desk.

Her eyes locked onto the black phone resting on the desk, and she hesitated for a moment before picking it up. With trembling fingers, she dialed her father's number. As it began to ring, Olivia took a seat, anxiously waiting for him to pick up.

"Hello?" said a familiar voice on the other end of the line.

"Dad, it's Olivia. Brian mentioned you called. Sounded serious. Everything okay?"

"Hey Livvy, how have you been? Are the king salmon starting to run yet?" he asked, his voice surprisingly casual.

"No, they're already done. We've hooked into several pinks lately, and I think the coho should be running any day now. Fishing has been red hot for everything else though." She paused for a moment, her hand now steady. "Dad, tell me what's up," she urged, growing impatient with his stalling.

There was a momentary silence on the other end of the line. "Olivia, I don't know how to say this, but I have some bad news." She heard him take a deep breath. "Grandma passed away this morning."

Olivia felt the air rush from her lungs, the weight of the news hitting her like a speeding freight train. Tears pooled around her eyes before spilling out onto her face. Her grandma had been her confidante, her rock, and her biggest supporter. She had helped her navigate through the hardest points in her life, and the thought of life without her seemed unimaginable. "Oh my God, Dad. What happened?"

"She passed away in her sleep. It was peaceful, at least," her dad replied, his voice heavy with sorrow, and she could tell he was holding back tears of his own.

Olivia fought to compose herself, but the tears kept flowing uncontrollably. "I can't believe she's gone. We were supposed to talk on Sunday," she said, her voice barely above a whisper. The pain of losing her grandma felt unbearable, and the suddenness of it all left her stunned and heartbroken.

"I know, Livvy, I know." His voice cracked. "We'll get through this together."

She wiped away her tears and exhaled, willing her tears to stop. "I'll be there for the funeral, of course. When is it?"

"Next Thursday morning. I talked to Brian, and he said it wasn't a problem."

"Okay. I'll talk to him about making arrangements to fly down as soon as I can. Thanks for letting me know, Dad," Olivia said, her voice still shaky.

"Of course, Livvy. Take care of yourself, okay?"

"I will. Love you," she said, ending the call before her dad could reply. She continued to sit in the solitude of the office, and she heard a couple chatting as they walked by. Her body was glued to the chair, and the immense weight of this loss permeated deep into her soul.

# 5

Brian's truck wobbled along the rutted dirt road, and Olivia bounced in her seat as they hit yet another pothole, causing her to spill the last remnants of her coffee onto the floorboard. With a sigh, she retrieved a napkin from her bag and wiped her floral mug clean before she stashed it away.

Lost in thought about the recent turn of events, she was caught off guard when Henry spoke. "Bumpy ride, huh?" She looked over to him.

After the conversation with her father, she'd spoken with Brian, who insisted she return home right away. With winter approaching and bookings dwindling, he mentioned the lodge would be fine if she left early. She had seen the reservations and knew he was lying, but she appreciated his intention to negate any potential guilt she might have for her premature departure. He also arranged a seat for her on a private plane heading to Seattle. From there, she'd catch a connecting flight to Billings, and a short drive from there would bring her to Red Lodge. To her grandma's house. Although saddened by the reality that she wouldn't be back any time soon, Brian assured her she would be welcomed back at the lodge the following season. Henry, her client from earlier in the week, was booked on the same flight. It would be nice to have a familiar face on the plane ride back, but she also didn't have much energy for small talk when she was so consumed in her grief.

"Indeed, it is," Olivia replied, gazing out the window at the passing scenery. "I had forgotten how rough this road is. This is actually my first time back into town this season."

"I can understand why," Henry remarked. "Leaving that lodge must be difficult." He shifted his attention towards Brian. "You've really built something special, Brian. And your fishing guides are top-notch, with Olivia being among the best I've ever had."

"Thank you, Henry," Brian said as he cranked the wheel, narrowly missing another pothole. "We will certainly miss her, but family always comes first." Olivia's face flushed at the unexpected attention.

"Hey Henry, how did the fishing downriver with Felix go the other day?" Olivia asked, eager to pivot the conversation away from herself.

"Well," he replied with a grin, "it depends on who you ask, me or the bears."

Olivia leaned in. "Did one of them get a little too close?" she asked playfully, imagining an intriguing encounter between Henry, Felix, and a couple of curious bears.

Henry let out a sigh. "Yeah, actually. Momma and her three cubs came running up to us. Before I knew it, Felix had his bear spray unloaded on her. Let me tell you, that stuff is nasty. It looked like she hit a trampoline the way she and those cubs stopped and ran back the other way. I couldn't imagine a pistol having the same effect."

"Yeah, bear spray can be a lifesaver in the wild. I had to use it a few times, and it's not a pleasant experience if the wind is blowing toward you."

Henry nodded and continued, "After the bear encounter, we decided to move on and hiked a mile downriver to a stunning pool. From atop the bluff, I spotted thousands of bright red salmon making their way upstream. I've never seen anything like it. I grabbed my phone and took a few photos." Henry took out his phone. "Oh, then, suddenly, we spotted three massive bears stepping out from the brush. They splashed and chased the fish all over the pool, occasionally catching a few. It was quite a sight to behold."

He swiped through the photos as he showed them to Olivia. "Wow, that's amazing! Too bad you couldn't fish there."

"That's exactly what Felix said too. But after a few moments of watching them, we decided the bears weren't leaving and we didn't want to risk another encounter. So, we just headed back to the lodge. Yesterday, I went out with Brian, and we floated the same section you and I passed. I caught a few good salmon, but it wasn't anything like that tributary you guided me to. I still can't believe that giant char I caught," Henry said with a hint of nostalgia.

He swiped over to the picture of him proudly holding the thirty-two-inch char. Olivia couldn't help but smile at that memory. "It was a great day, wasn't it?"

Henry chuckled, admiring the photo. "Sure was. You're just a better guide than ol' Felix," he teased.

Olivia grinned. "That's not the first time I've heard that. But at least Felix tries."

"I'm sorry to hear you have to head back, Olivia," Henry said in a gentle tone. "Brian mentioned something about a family member, but he didn't give much detail. It's okay if you don't want to talk about it, but I just wanted to express my condolences."

Olivia glanced down at the spilt coffee below her feet and decided to opened up, sharing the details of her grandma's passing and her plans to return to Montana for the funeral, followed by an extended stay for the winter.

"I'm sorry for your loss. Were you two close?"

"We were. She was my rock during a tough time a few years ago. I'll never forget how much she helped me through it. If it weren't for her, I never would have met Brian. She introduced me to him through a mutual friend, and that's how I ended up out here."

"It sounds like she was an incredible woman," Henry commented.

"She was."

The remainder of the ride was relatively uneventful, with the occasional small talk and fishing tales, until they arrived at the secluded riverside airport reserved for private planes.

"Here we are," Brian announced as he parked the truck and stepped out to unload bags.

Henry got out and Olivia trailed behind him. "Thank you for the amazing trip, Brian. It was quite an experience, and I hope to come back soon. Maybe I can even convince my son to come with me next time."

Brian shook his hand before handing over his bag. "We'd love to have you back anytime. It was a pleasure having you. Have a safe trip home, and congratulations on the upcoming grandbaby."

Brian then retrieved Olivia's large bag and hugged her before handing it over. "We'll miss you up here. Take care of yourself and your family, and we'll see you next year."

"Absolutely, Brian. I'll be back before you know it. Good luck with the rest of the season. You're going to need it."

Brian chuckled and nodded his head in agreement. He climbed back into his pickup, rolled his window down, and waved as he drove out of the parking lot and back toward the lodge.

Olivia was unfamiliar with this private airport as she had always traveled through the larger airport in King Salmon. However, Brian liked to go the extra mile to enhance his guests' experiences and had arranged a direct flight to Seattle for Henry with a local pilot named Terry. Since Terry had an extra seat, he offered it to Olivia for free as a gesture of gratitude for the business Brian had brought him over the years. This saved a considerable amount of time and money compared to the traditional route, and Olivia was thrilled as she was scheduled to be back home to Montana by midnight.

"Do you know where we should go?" Olivia asked Henry, confused by the casual setting and lack of signs.

"Yeah, our plane is just down there, behind the man sitting on the bench in the suit." Henry pointed out a small prop plane tied next to a dock a hundred feet away. The plane appeared aged, with peeling paint in some areas and rust starting to take over.

"Are you sure it's safe?"

Henry laughed. "First time flying private, and you're already a connoisseur?"

"It just looks old and run down. Like the kind of car you give to a teenager. You know, the kind that sometimes starts, is littered with scratches and dents, and you fully expect it to die on you at any moment?"

"I know exactly what you're talking about. We gave my son one of those. A '96 Ford Taurus. I want to say it was blue, but there were so many scratches and rust that I couldn't tell." He laughed. "But this plane is fine. I had a great flight on the way up here with no issues at all. Nothing to be worried about."

The two approached the dock and settled down on the open bench across from the plane. Terry, the pilot, had not yet arrived, and there was no one there to greet them except for the man in the suit, who glanced away as they sat down. Olivia took a deep breath, trying to ease her nerves, and reminded herself of Henry's words. She hoped their flight would be uneventful and safe—nothing to be worried about.

# 6

Terry slammed the snooze button on his alarm clock and finally dragged himself out of bed. His head throbbed from the whiskey he drank the night before, and his eyes struggled to focus in the bright morning light. Feeling the consequences of his rowdy night, he stumbled to the bathroom, swirled some mouthwash, and jumped in the shower, hoping to wash away the remnants of his intoxicated state.

After sifting through piles of clothes scattered around his room to find a clean shirt, he settled on one that barely smelled of cigarette smoke with only one noticeable stain. As he hastily tried to put it on, he realized he had it on backward and corrected it. While he was inadvertently trying to push his head through the armhole, a loud bang on the door startled him.

"Terry, get up! You said you'd meet me at the diner forty-five minutes ago," a familiar voice shouted from the other side.

Terry groaned as he managed to put on his shirt, unlock the deadbolt, and open the front door to his trailer. Owen, his copilot, stood with a heavy sigh and arms crossed. "You said you'd meet me at the diner forty-five minutes ago."

Terry smiled as he replied, "I know, but did you bring me breakfast?"

Unfazed, Owen handed him a to-go box filled with elk sausage, pancakes, and a thermos full of coffee. "One of these days, I'm going to catch on to you, and then who will bring you breakfast?" Owen grumbled and pushed past him toward the bathroom.

Terry cleared a pile of bills and other junk off the table to make room for his to-go box. He grabbed a black-and-red flannel and took a quick sniff before slipping it over his shirt. Sitting down and taking a sip from his thermos, he called out to Owen across the trailer, "How many do we have today?"

Owen's voice echoed through the bathroom door. "Just three. One of Brian's guides, who I guess is scared of winter so she's bailing early; one of his guests; and that one guy in a suit who met with the mayor yesterday."

Owen emerged from the bathroom, looking refreshed and ready to go. "It's a four-hour flight back to Seattle and another four back. I really want to stop at that Mexican place for lunch, so let's get on with it," he said with a hint of annoyance still in his voice.

"Let me eat my breakfast first, Owen. It's barely hot as it is. Can you imagine what it would be like if I waited until we got to the plane?"

Owen sighed and leaned against the counter. "That's why we were supposed to meet at the diner."

"We have plenty of time, even enough time to grab a bite in Seattle. I'm thinking we should try that new Chinese joint instead though," Terry snickered.

Owen scowled. "Stop messing with me. Today's not the day for it."

"Fine, fine. Did you get the extra boxes loaded into the plane already?" Terry said in a more serious tone.

Owen let out his breath and sat next to him. "Yeah, I got the boxes loaded last night. They are all secure and ready to go. Did you call you-know-who?"

"Relax, Owen. It's all handled. I made the call last night. It'll all be taken care of while we're getting some fried rice and orange chicken," he said, grinning.

Owen stood up, his face flushed with anger, and glared at Terry. Terry held up his hands. "I'm just kidding, buddy. We're having tacos, and everything is set up. No need to worry."

Terry grabbed his daypack from a neighboring chair and tossed it at Owen. "Start the truck. I'll be out in a minute. I want to enjoy the warmth of my heated seat as soon as I sit down."

Owen caught the half-zipped pack and shot Terry a puzzled glance, raising an eyebrow in disbelief. An assortment of jerky, nuts, and an emergency kit tumbled to the floor before Owen could zip up the bag and nonchalantly kicked the items below the table. "Heated seats? When did you add those to your junker?"

Terry didn't bother to answer. Instead, he took a satisfied gulp from his thermos and waved dismissively at Owen, signaling him to head out. Owen shrugged and exited the door to fire up the worn-out truck parked in front of Terry's trailer.

As soon as the door shut, Terry walked over to his closet, his eyes scanning the stacks of cardboard boxes that filled it. He quickly rummaged through the top box and retrieved a handful of cash, stuffing it into his pocket. While grabbing his coat, the hanger slipped from the collar and rattled against the floor. He kicked it aside without a second thought, slammed the closet door behind him, and went outside to the truck.

Terry opened the passenger door and glanced at Owen. "Where's my bag?" Owen reached for his coat, which was covering the bag, and patted it.

"Good, you managed not to mess that up. Let's get going."

"One of these days, Terry, you're going to push too hard." Owen shifted the truck into drive and headed toward the docks.

<h1 style="text-align:center">7</h1>

Olivia heard the rumbling of a truck engine as it approached the dock. Peering over, she observed the approaching, beat-up vehicle. It was covered in a thick layer of dirt, but she could still make out the rust surrounding the wheel wells. The dents in the door were also visible, even through the grime. She watched as it parked and two men hopped out. She assumed the older of the two was Terry, who was in his late forties and had a tall, lean build. He wore a black-and-red flannel button-up, jeans, and cowboy boots. His unkempt gray beard and hair matched his worn appearance. A blue baseball cap sat atop his head, but she couldn't make out the logo.

The younger man was in his mid-twenties, wearing blue jeans and black tennis shoes paired with a stained gray sweatshirt. His attempt to grow a beard was unsuccessful, and a red baseball cap held back his dark blond hair. Olivia assumed he was either Terry's hired hand or copilot, although she wasn't certain a copilot was necessary for such a small plane. Either way, their appearance did not help relieve any of her initial hesitations.

"Owen! Load their bags on the plane," Terry commanded as they descended to the dock and approached Olivia, Henry, and the man in the suit.

"Hello, my name is Terry, and this is my copilot, Owen." Terry gestured to the younger man who was reaching for their bags. "We'll bring you back to Seattle this morning, but don't expect any free sodas or peanuts. This is not that type of flight. This is also not the type of flight that has a bathroom, and with an estimated airtime of four hours, you'd better go now," Terry stated as he pointed toward the bathrooms by the entrance of the docks.

Henry jumped up from the bench and said, "Thanks for the reminder, Terry. I'll be right back."

Olivia stood up to exchange pleasantries with Terry, but her introduction was intercepted when the man in the suit stepped in front of her to shake Terry's hand.

"Lee, how was your trip?" Terry asked.

"Not great. Unfortunately, things aren't moving in the right direction, but that's never stopped me before. You'll be seeing more of me, it seems."

"We'll take the business," Terry said as Lee walked past him to the open door of the plane. While at the fishing lodge, Olivia had heard guests mentioning Terry as quite the character. It was never anything unsettling, just a common theme that he was rough around the edges.

Olivia approached him again and the two shook hands. As she was about to introduce herself, Terry beat her to it. "Olivia, I hear you're scared of a little snow," he said, a sly grin on his face.

When Olivia and Brian discussed her situation and having to leave early, she'd asked him to be discreet. It seemed he respected that, and she presumed Terry was fishing for a reason.

"Yup, this Montana girl sure does hate a little snow," she retorted. Terry chuckled but didn't push the subject more as he gestured toward the plane. It was time to load up.

As she approached the plane's door, she noticed once again how worn it looked. The rivets around the window had begun to rust, just like the hinges. So when she reached for the support handle, she wasn't surprised when it slightly jiggled in its place.

The interior of the plane matched the upkeep standards of the exterior. The cockpit held two faded, cracked light-blue leather pilot seats. In the passenger section, there were four stained, white faux-leather bucket seats next to each window separated by a burnt orange carpet runner with a matching roof, giving off an early 1980's vibe.

Behind the seats was a shoddy shelving system with a rotomolded cooler in the middle. Olivia guessed the cooler was used to transport freshly harvested fish and game like caribou or moose. There were a few smaller passenger bags, a maroon bag labeled "Mail," and some cardboard boxes on the shelves. The rest of the area was used to store the passengers' larger bags. She took note of her large duffel and smaller daypack on the shelf.

Olivia surveyed the three seats available and chose the one in front of Lee on the far side of the door because it appeared to be the least worn-out option. As she settled into her seat and continued to take in her surroundings, she caught Henry missing a step and stumbling as he walked onto the plane. "I'm fine!" he exclaimed with a laugh and sat beside her.

"I'm going to miss this place. What an experience," Henry said. Olivia nodded and smiled politely but didn't offer more.

She glanced out the window and observed Owen refueling the plane and checking all the equipment. Next to him, Terry leisurely smoked a cigarette and watched.

Once Terry finished his cigarette and flicked it into the water, he climbed into the pilot's seat. With his door still ajar, he yelled at Owen to hurry up. Owen quickly finished up and jumped in, taking his seat next to Terry. "Are we ready?" he asked.

Terry glared over as he slammed his door shut. "You tell me, Mr. Copilot."

Owen picked up his clipboard and turned to Terry, running through the checklist. "Bags loaded, check. Plane fueled, check. Passengers briefed and boarded, check. Equipment tested, check. Flight logged, check. Everything on my end is done. How was your smoke, Terry?"

"It was great! Thanks for asking."

Olivia could sense the tension between the two. Terry motioned to start the plane. As Owen turned the key, Olivia could hear a whining and grinding sound as the engine attempted to start, filling the cabin with the stench of burnt jet fuel. Owen flipped the key again, hoping for a different result, but nothing changed.

With a look of disappointment, Terry opened his door and stepped outside, leaving a bewildered Owen in the cockpit. Moments later, he returned, turned the key himself, and the engine immediately fired up.

"What was it?" Owen asked.

"Only something we covered yesterday and twenty times before that."

Owen frowned and turned away. Olivia's eyes met Terry's as he glanced back and to the others. "Ready or not, we're Seattle bound!"

Olivia's chest tightened now that takeoff seemed imminent. The idea of flying in such a small, rustic plane with two bickering pilots made her feel uncertain. However, as she looked around the plane, she tried to reassure herself, knowing that all of the other passengers had arrived via Terry's flight service. As well as the majority of the guests at the lodge. That helped calm her nerves, but they weren't settled.

Terry revved the engine a few more times, causing the entire plane to shake. Olivia gripped the armrests of her seat and stared out the window as they slowly began to taxi into open water. She could feel the vibration of the floats beneath her as the plane accelerated. The plane bounced as it raced down the river and suddenly lifted off the water. Olivia felt momentarily nauseated as her stomach dropped while the plane ascended higher and higher into the air.

Looking out of the window, she could see the rugged Alaskan wilderness below. She noted several of her favorite fishing holes on the Naknek River and could even make out the small tributary she had taken Malcolm, Zoey, and Henry to.

As they continued to climb, Terry announced from the front seat, "Lady and gentlemen, we are now cruising at an altitude of ten thousand feet. Hopefully, you all peed beforehand; if not, we will be in Seattle in four hours. You can use the toilet then."

Henry turned to Olivia and made a face. She grinned back before settling back into her seat, still trying to shake off the lingering nerves. The rhythmic hum of the engine helped, slowly lulling her into a peaceful sleep.

# 8

Intense turbulence jolted Olivia awake. She rubbed the sleep from her eyes and peered out the window, trying to make out the land below. Dark and dense clouds obscured her view. Henry was also slowly awakening. Their eyes met, and without a word, he gave a subtle shrug.

She cast a quick glance into the pilot's cabin and saw Terry and Owen locked in a heated dispute. The roar of the engines drowned out most of their words, leaving her with only parts of the exchange. She made out a few insults directed toward Owen before she heard the word "storm."

Growing more concerned with each passing moment, she leaned into the cockpit and asked the pilots, "What's going on?"

Terry briefly turned back to her and rubbed his neck. "Nothing. Nothing at all."

She was skeptical as Terry turned back and snapped another muffled remark to Owen. Unbuckling her seat belt, she stepped into the cockpit, her voice firm. "Are we flying into a storm?"

Terry's eyes widened in surprise when he saw her beside him. He tightened his grip on the controls before forcing a smile. "No need to worry, ma'am. I've flown this route hundreds of times before."

"I don't believe that. You two look like fish out of water up here. What's going on?"

Terry took a deep breath as he turned in his chair to face her, saying, "Nothing's wrong. We just have a minor situation developing. You'll be the first to know if it becomes anything more than that."

Sighing, Olivia returned to her seat and fastened her seat belt again. Despite Terry's reassurance, she shifted in her seat, trying her best to get comfortable. Her eyes scanned every detail of the cabin until her gaze fell to the window. The nearby mountains were now visible, but dark clouds in the distance reminded her of the large snow squalls she'd become accustomed to growing up. A sense of unease gnawed at her. They were in for a rough ride.

The plane initiated a gentle leftward tilt away from the direction of the storm. It didn't seem to help. The turbulence intensified, and the plane's movements became increasingly erratic. Olivia's knuckles whitened as she clutched the armrest. She glanced at her fellow passengers. Henry's eyes were squeezed shut, his grasp on the armrests tightening with each jolt. Lee sat wide-eyed and breathless, his attention fixed on the passing clouds outside his window. Olivia tried to offer a reassuring smile, but Lee remained oblivious to it.

Time passed slowly, but the storm continued to close in, causing the cabin to darken. Terry lifted the right side of his headset, dabbing at the sweat gathering by his ear, while Owen attempted to hide his constant fidgeting. Olivia sensed something was amiss. She leaned in closer to the cockpit to determine what was happening.

Terry shouted at Owen, "How could you be so careless? Preparing this plane has been your job for the past three years. That includes checking the weather! Do you have any idea how massive this storm is?" Terry's face was beet red with anger as sweat collected over his eyebrows.

Owen trembled in his chair, his face ghostly white as he attempted to respond. He stuttered, "I d-d-did check the paper this morning. I checked it at breakfast.

The forecast is clear all day today. Tomorrow, they're expecting a big storm though." Owen reached down to the floor and picked up a crumbled newspaper, pointing at it as he explained.

Terry snatched the newspaper from his grip and scanned it. His anger intensified when he realized the truth. "I can't believe this, Owen! It's Wednesday!" Terry yelled. His voice echoed through the tense cabin. "This is yesterday's paper!"

Owen was speechless. His tremors ceased and he froze. As the weight of his mistake sank in, he became visibly altered by the gravity of the situation. Olivia noticed the distress on his face and felt a mix of sympathy and anger. *How did he mess up the day?*

Terry took two deep breaths to control his frustration. With a calm but stern voice, he wiped the moisture from his forehead and yelled over the noise of the engine, "Well, how big of a storm is this, Owen? We've been trying to avoid it for fifteen minutes now, and it's still heading right toward us."

Owen grabbed the newspaper from Terry's hand and flipped back to the weather section. He let out a heavy sigh before finally managing to speak. "Big," was all Olivia managed to understand, his voice barely above a whisper.

Terry's voice echoed throughout the plane as he glanced over his shoulder and shouted, "Lady and gentlemen, I regret to inform you that our copilot has made a serious mistake, and we now find ourselves flying into a massive snowstorm. Please remain seated and brace yourselves for some nasty turbulence. I will do my best to navigate through this safely, but I won't sugarcoat it—it's going to be a rough ride."

Olivia's heart raced as her sweaty palms strangled the armrest. The turbulence intensified, and she could feel the small plane being thrashed by the intense winds. She tried to calm herself down by taking deep breaths, but the fear was overwhelming. Thoughts of worst-case scenarios flooded her mind, and she couldn't shake the feeling of impending disaster.

As she looked around the cabin, she recognized the same fear in Henry. His face was tense, with beads of sweat forming around his forehead. He managed to wipe it with one hand, but the other remained tightly gripped to the armrest.

He turned to her, seeking a bit of reassurance. "This is normal, right? These storms happen all the time, don't they?"

The question brought Olivia out of her trance, prompting her to recall the minimal survival training she had acquired throughout her life. Determined to stay calm and think clearly, she steadied her breath and responded to him with a serious tone, "Yeah, storms happen all the time, but this one does look bad. It'll be okay though. It might get a little dicey for a bit, but we'll all be okay."

Henry nodded, absorbing the gravity of the situation. But before he could respond, the plane jerked aggressively, bouncing up and down several times, leaving a sense of dread lingering in the air.

Loud beeping erupted from the cockpit, sending a chill down Olivia's spine. Her heart rate quickened, and she exchanged another worried glance with Henry, unable to hide her fear from him any longer.

"Air control, this is flight TS522 en route to Seattle. We are experiencing severe weather and need to land as soon as possible." Terry's voice cut through the cacophony of the plane. "Air control, can you read… Air control, can you hear me?"

Olivia glanced at Henry once more. His face was pale and frozen in place and his eyes locked on Terry. He hadn't moved a muscle since his last comment. She reached across the aisle and placed a reassuring hand on his shoulder, conveying some sense of comfort amid the chaos.

Realizing she hadn't heard anything from Lee, she spun around to face him. He was also staring at Terry while his face glistened with sweat. His hands tightly gripped the armrests, and his mouth hung wide open in shock. He seemed absorbed in the unfolding situation, unaware or unable to acknowledge her presence.

"Owen, find me a spot to land this plane immediately!" Terry yelled.

"If we can just get past these next couple of mountains, I know there's a large, flat tundra we can put the plane down on," Owen said.

Terry's demeanor intensified as he shouted with rage, "I said right now! We can't make it fifty more miles in this storm."

Owen's eyes widened as he focused on the map, his finger tracing different routes with increased urgency. "Oh no…there's nothing," he finally concluded.

"Nothing? Should I go ahead and crash into the side of the mountain now, or can you find me somewhere to land?"

"I don't know what to do, Terry. I've searched the map, and there's nothing. Do you want to look?"

Terry's frustration boiled over as he snatched the map from his hand. "Take the controls. I'll figure it out. Try not to crash in the meantime. Is that something you can handle?"

Owen clenched his jaw and seized the controls.

After a quick moment with the map, Terry regained command of the plane and veered sharply to the left before tossing the map at Owen.

In a composed manner, Terry addressed the passengers, "Everyone, listen. We are going to make an emergency landing. I've identified a small lake deep in the mountains, and it's our best chance for a safe landing. Please hold on tight and brace yourselves. I'll do my best to land this aircraft safely, but prepare yourself for anything."

Terry scanned the cabin, meeting the anxious gazes of the passengers. "If anything goes wrong, there will be water, and it will be cold. If that happens, grab your life jackets and make your way to the shore. Stick together, stay calm, and we'll get through this."

Olivia replayed the events leading up to this moment in her mind. She had been hesitant about flying in a small plane, especially in Alaska's unpredictable weather, but Brian had assured her Terry was an experienced pilot. It would also save her time compared to the commercial jet option too, so she went for it. She fully regretted that decision now.

She let out a deep breath to steady her nerves and remembered the floats on the plane. Maybe, just maybe, it would be straightforward to land and take off once the storm passed. That thought gave her hope.

Henry was still frozen in place. He noticed her looking this time and returned a quick glance before fixating on the cockpit once more. "It'll be okay, Henry. Trust that it will be okay," she stated, trying to calm him down. But it didn't work. He remained tense, so she redirected her attention out the window.

She noticed a long, slender lake that she assumed was their destination. Large trees encircled it with a narrow rock beach, but she spotted a few clusters of massive rocks among the foliage. She made a mental note of the two towering peaks on either side of the lake. Despite the situation, she couldn't help but appreciate the picturesque scenery. It would have been a beautiful spot to visit under different circumstances. *The fishing is probably great.*

The aircraft began circling the mountain lake, gradually descending after each pass. Olivia lost count of the number of circles they made but noticed when the plane straightened out. As they descended further, the plane violently shook from side to side. Terry jolted it up and veered right, leaving Olivia confused. He looped the plane back around and resumed a descent toward the lake, the plane still shaking as it descended.

The longest moment of Olivia's life passed as the plane approached the water. Her nerves were at an all-time high, but she took one more deep breath and reminded herself of the plane's floats. *It'll be just like any other landing.* She double-checked her seat belt, ensured her boots were tied, and gripped the armrest, locking her gaze on the shore outside her window.

As the plane was about to touch down, she felt a sudden jolt to the left. Out of the corner of her eye, she saw debris flying by outside the window. Before she could react, the plane overcorrected to the right and miraculously remained upright as it slid sideways across the water until it came to a stop. A few seconds passed before Olivia was startled by a cold chill racing over her foot. She looked down to find water seeping and trickling across the floor of the plane.

# 9

Water now gushed into the cabin, numbing Olivia's senses to the point she almost missed Terry shouting, "Get out!" His door flung open, and he plunged into the water with his backpack in hand.

"Time to go!" Owen shouted before he disappeared from the cockpit as well.

Olivia unbuckled her seat belt as the frigid water poured over her lap. She stood up and noticed Henry yanking on his belt.

"What's wrong, Henry? We need to go," she said, attempting to keep her composure, but panic was setting in. They had crash-landed in a remote lake, and she had no idea if they were still in Alaska or had crossed into Canada. But none of that mattered. All she knew was the lake water was freezing. It would soon fill the plane's cabin, and both pilots had abandoned them.

Henry's eyes were wide with panic. "It's stuck, I can't get it undone."

While Olivia processed Henry's situation, she spotted Lee prying open the cabin door. Lee leaped out of sight without offering a helping hand or word.

Olivia took several shallow breaths to compose herself before reaching down into the frigid water to help Henry. She tried unbuckling it once, twice, and then four more times without any luck. It was jammed shut. It might have broken from the impact of the landing but more likely from neglect.

Henry looked up at her, the water now to his chest. "Olivia, help. There's got to be something you can do," he pleaded, tears streaming down his face.

Olivia took another deep breath as her daypack floated by her. *Of course.* She grabbed it and unzipped the pocket, pulled out a pocketknife, and showed it to Henry.

"My savior," he said, nodding in relief. Olivia reached down in the water once more to the base of the seat belt and, with one swipe, cut the strap. Henry instantly popped up out of his chair, just as the water was reaching his chin.

"Thank you! Thank you!" He embraced Olivia in a bear hug. Tears poured from her eyes as well. She just saved Henry's life, something she had failed to do in the past with the man she cared for most.

"Time to go, Henry," she said, breaking away and orienting him in the frame of the door. Without hesitation, he swiftly jumped out through the door.

As the plane's cabin began to roll, Olivia steadied herself from the shifting floor by gripping Henry's chair with one hand while securing the knife in her front pocket with the other. After fastening her pack, she followed Henry, making her way through the rising plane door and plunging into the open water.

As she plummeted into the water, the sinking plane dragged her under. Wrestling against the weight of her wet clothes and pack, she struggled to reach the surface. Kicking and thrashing, she felt the water's cold touch overwhelm her. Her vision dimmed until a hand brushed against her head. She desperately reached for it, only to be lifted to the surface by her pack.

"I've got you. Stay still," Henry said. She obeyed as air filled her lungs with an initial breath as Henry found a balanced position that allowed them both to stabilize on their backs.

"You saved my life. I thought I was going to drown," she said as she gulped for air.

"You saved my life too. When everyone else bailed, you put yourself in danger and stuck with me. I'm not leaving you. We'll make it out of here, together."

Olivia nodded, her warm tears mixing with the frigid lake water covering her face.

"Look," Henry said as he turned and pointed toward the plane. Its entire cabin was now submerged, the nose leading the descent until only the tail was visible above the water's surface. In a matter of seconds, the lake swallowed the aircraft and seamlessly settled back to its original condition as though the crash had never occurred.

"Which way did the others go?" Olivia asked through chattering teeth. "We need to get to shore, fast."

"I don't know," Henry said, scanning the turbulent waters around them.

Just then, Olivia discerned faint yelling over the crashing waves. "Wait, listen. Someone's yelling."

"Where's it coming from?"

Olivia closed her eyes and focused on the sound. She tried to tune out everything else and concentrate on the distant voice. As the yelling continued, she was certain it was coming from behind them. She turned and made out a lone figure jumping on a large boulder and flailing his arms.

"There, Henry. Over there. Let's go."

The waves continued to toss their bodies aimlessly, and they took in mouthfuls of water as they struggled to make their way toward the boulder. In time, the duo learned to move as one, timing their breaths and swim strokes with the frequency of the waves.

Olivia could feel her hands stiffen in the cold water and her mobility became more robotic. She glanced at her right hand and noticed her fingertips had turned a ghostly white. "Henry, are we close? It's cold."

She felt him turn his body to check behind them before replying, "Twenty more yards. We've got this."

*I can do that.* She started thrashing her legs once more. Moments later, Terry grabbed her by the arms and dragged her across a rocky shore. Closing her eyes, she let the world continue without her as she gave in to the exhaustion. An occasional muffled voice nudged her consciousness, but nothing could lure her back to reality.

An intense burning in her fingertips slowly brought her back. She focused on them as the blood returned. The same sensation arose in her boots. It retreated, and a sense of relief rushed over her mind.

She had escaped the plane and made it to shore. However, she knew this was only the beginning. The ache in her fingers and toes quickly hushed her celebratory moment and reminded her that they needed a fire soon to survive the night.

Olivia opened her eyes and gazed at the towering spruce trees accentuating the darkening skies as large storm clouds settled over the lake. *This storm is going to be nasty.*

Terry's voice startled her. "Olivia, are you okay?"

Henry stood beside Terry, but no sign of Lee or Owen. She assumed they would have made it to shore by now. "I'm fine," she said. She made eye contact with Henry and then glanced at Terry. "How are you two?"

They both nodded their heads.

"Where's Owen and Lee? Did they make it back to shore yet?"

"Owen is down the shore. The idiot said he had an idea, so when I saw you two swimming to shore, I left him to come help. I haven't seen Lee though. Did he make it out of the plane?" Terry asked.

With a bewildered look, Henry turned to Olivia and said, "Yeah, he left right before us."

Olivia stood up, unbuckled her pack, and sauntered onto the boulder where she spotted Terry earlier, hoping for a better view. She scanned the water for Lee but didn't see any sign of him. The waves continued to surge higher and higher with the incoming storm. Finally, as she looked up the shore, she spotted two hands waving erratically.

"Lee!" She yelled, pointing out the hands to the others before sprinting up shore. She was unsure if the others were following her, but as soon as she reached Lee's position, she dove into the lake. Despite feeling fatigued from earlier, she was more balanced and confident without the weight of her pack. Within seconds, she was by Lee's side.

"Relax, I've got you. Turn onto your back, and I'll bring you to shore."

She was surprised when she heard another voice next to her say, "We've got you." Henry was in the water beside her, extending his arms out to support Lee. She nodded her thanks while they carefully guided Lee toward the beach.

Once there, Terry and Owen helped them out of the water.

Olivia once again collapsed on the rocky shoreline. "I'm cold, wet, and exhausted. Please tell me you have a plan?"

Terry knelt next to her before he addressed the group, "During our flyover, I spotted a large grouping of rocks nestled in the trees. There should be an overhang where we can shelter under to escape the storm. Let's all head that way and get a fire going. We can warm up and figure out what to do next."

"Works for me," Henry chimed in.

"Terry, I told you I'd get a shelter set up. I'm building a lean-to over in the trees. It's big enough for all of us," Owen said. "We just talked about this."

Olivia looked down the shore and could make out the beginnings of Owen's lean-to. After a quick assessment, she deemed the unknown rocky formation a better option. "I agree. The rock formation is worth checking out. Where was it, Terry?"

"It's close. Down the shore toward your pack and inland five, maybe six hundred yards."

Owen threw his hands up and turned to leave the others. He took two steps before looking back and said, "I'm heading back to my lean-to. You're all welcome to join me, including you, Terry." He then walked away. To Olivia's surprise, Lee stood up and joined him and the two headed down to the beach.

"Let's get out of here." Terry strolled the opposite way of Owen. Henry shrugged and followed, with Olivia closely behind him. She grabbed her pack as she passed and continued down the shoreline before cutting off into the dense brush and timber.

# 10

The trio trekked through an old game trail, passing thick brush and canopy that served as a shield from the gusts of cold air the storm brought in. As they approached the rock formation, Olivia spotted a pile of dry, dead branches just off the trail that she knew she should collect. Henry turned back and watched her, his face perplexed, trying to decipher the reason.

"I'm wet and freezing. We need a fire. Might as well gather dry wood when we see it," she explained.

Terry noticed and nodded in agreement. "Good call. Once we find a spot in the rocks, I'll start working on the fire. I have waterproof matches in my pack, so it shouldn't take long." He reached down to pick up a handful of branches from the ground. Henry did as well.

As Olivia trudged along with her arms loaded with firewood, she barely noticed her surroundings until the thick canopy began to retreat into a large clearing. Three massive granite rock formations dominated the center and were surrounded by many smaller boulders. One of the larger rocks leaned over, resting on another, and behind them, a stack of large boulders blocked the area in. It was the perfect place for a camp, sheltered from the oncoming rain, snow, and wind.

Olivia gazed at the rock formation and felt something inside of her let go. *We made it. This is our spot.*

Terry walked into the opening and placed his woodpile and pack down on the ground. "This will do," he said as he observed his surroundings.

As Henry and Olivia joined him, Henry turned to Olivia. "Wow, this place is breathtaking. If we hadn't just survived a plane crash, being wet, cold, and stranded, I'd probably really enjoy this place."

"Agreed," she replied, attempting to embrace his optimism. When she walked toward Terry, she noticed him fumbling to get a small container out of his pack.

"Need a hand?" she asked, crouching beside him.

He hesitated but said, "Yeah, that would be great," and handed his pack over. "My hands are a bit shaky. They just need to warm up."

After taking out a small plastic container from Terry's bag, she found some dry kindling in it, along with a pack of waterproof matches. Olivia put those to the side and cleared a small area of leaves and rocks from under the large overhang. Once she arranged a circular formation using a few small stones, she carefully stacked a handful of twigs within the fire ring, creating a structure closely resembling a miniature log cabin.

"Good thing you brought this, Terry," she said as she prepared the kindling.

"I don't go anywhere without it because if you can't make fire out here, you're dead. Usually, I have some sort of food stashed in there too, but I must have forgotten it."

Olivia struck a match against the striking strip on the side of the matchbox and carefully placed it on top of the kindling. It instantly erupted. Flame engulfed the wooden structure, and she smelled the familiar scent of burning timber as smoke billowed out. She added more sticks to the fire, cautiously arranging them to keep the flames well-vented. Soon, the fire was large enough to feel its warm embrace.

"Well done, Olivia," Henry said as he rubbed his hands together, absorbing the heat of the fire. Terry nodded in acknowledgment.

"Thanks, I've made a few of these in my day," she said, smiling as the memory of James's first fire flooded her mind. She could feel his joy radiating through her, offering much-needed comfort.

***

They had been spending a lot of time together, and her initial butterflies had developed into strong feelings. Though they hadn't officially labeled their relationship yet, she couldn't imagine a day without his warm smile or his playful kindness. He had a way about him that brought her serenity.

She had convinced him to go on a backpacking trip to an alpine lake in the Beartooth Mountains, a lake she had never been to before. Despite her unfamiliarity, she had heard from numerous sources that it was overflowing with trout.

Olivia had grown up backpacking, so the trip was just another weekend excursion for her. However, James was hesitant to join her. "What's wrong? Why don't you want to go?"

"It's not that I don't want to go. I just have work on Monday, and I don't want to wear myself out," he had told her.

Knowing James well enough at this point, she saw through his excuse and called him out on it. "James, you're an intern at an engineering office. You sit at a desk all day. Come on, I've already borrowed a pack and sleeping bag for you. Just come, please?"

The hike up to the lake with James had been amazing, and they ended up catching a ton of fish. But when it came time to set up camp and cook dinner, things got interesting. She had asked him which one he preferred. His face sank as he searched for a response. After a few seconds, she pushed him, "James, do you want to set up the tent or start the fire?"

"Ahh, hmm, I don't know, Olivia. Which would you prefer?" he responded, seemingly satisfied that he had finally come up with an answer.

"Wait, you know how to do both, don't you?"

James's face turned bright red as he averted his attention toward a passing cloud. "What? Of course I do. I'll set up the tent, and you do the fire, okay?"

Olivia kissed him before she sat down by the fire ring and watched as he walked toward their packs. He pulled out his sleeping bag, and released it from its stuff sack. He then shook the bag and checked inside, ensuring it was empty.

Olivia observed with intrigue. Typically, she would set up the tent first and then place her air mattress and sleeping bag inside. She had never seen this approach before and was curious how it would play out.

James picked up the sleeping bag and patted it from one end to the other as if searching for something. With a look of befuddlement, he turned to Olivia. "Bad news. I think we forgot to pack the poles."

She began laughing hysterically. "That's the sleeping bag, James. Not the tent."

"Well, that's something, I guess," he said, scratching his head as he looked down at the sprawled-out bag.

Olivia couldn't stop laughing. James just stared back at her until she collected herself. "Here, you make the fire. I'll set up the tent," she said, handing him a fire starter and lighter.

James hesitantly took them from her but didn't move. She noticed and asked, "Do you know how?"

He shook his head.

"James, you don't know how to set up a tent, you don't know how to start a fire… Is this your first time camping?"

"Of course it is, Olivia! I grew up in Nebraska. There are no mountains to camp in there." He gestured with his hand in the air, then rubbed it through his hair. "That's the only reason I was hesitant to go on this trip. I needed some time to research how to do this stuff. Will you help me instead of just laughing at me?"

"Okay, okay, I'll give you a pass. You're lucky you're cute. Of course I'll help." With a smirk, she grabbed his hand and led him down to the fire ring. After explaining where the fire should go, she snatched a few small sticks and set them up like a log cabin. "Fires need two things: fuel and air. Stacking the sticks like this allows plenty of air in so the fire can burn the fuel."

Olivia grabbed her fire starter and placed it in the middle of the wooden structure before handing James the lighter. "Now, just light it."

James did, and the kindling erupted. It slowly grew larger, and James's grin grew to match. He then leaned in and gave her a gentle kiss. As he broke away, he whispered, "Thank you."

***

Olivia replied, "You're welcome," as she snapped back to reality, remembering she was stranded in the remote wilderness with no way to escape. She was surrounded by two rather confused men, wondering why she was now talking to herself instead of enjoying their time in the Beartooth Mountain range and embracing the man she had grown to love.

# 11

"We're running low on firewood," Terry said, breaking the silence that had settled over the group while they huddled for warmth around the dwindling flames.

Olivia's teeth chattered as she felt the chill seeping through her wet clothes. She had been so focused on trying to warm up that she hadn't realized how low their supply of firewood had gotten.

"We can't let the fire die," she muttered.

Henry, who was hunched over with his arms wrapped tightly around himself, spoke through episodes of uncontrollable shivering. "I'm still wet and cold. This fire isn't working. What else can we do?"

Olivia felt the same way. She was freezing and the feeble fire did little to warm her up. She knew hypothermia was a real threat in their situation, and they needed to act fast. Then it clicked.

"Of course," she said. "We have to wring our clothes out. We won't get warm if we stay wet like this."

Olivia hesitated as her eyes scanned the circle of men surrounding her. She was accustomed to being the only woman in any given situation, but she became instantly aware of that at this moment. She watched as each one of them undressed without a second thought and set their clothes beside the fire. The relief overtook their faces as warmth finally took hold of them. She knew she would have to do the same and decided modesty was not something she was inclined to at this time.

She quickly stripped down to her underwear and wrung out her clothes before laying them on the rocks surrounding the fire to dry. She did the same with her socks, placing them on top of her boots. Her clothes immediately began to steam and she felt the warmth from the flames seep deep into her muscles. If her clothes dried before dark, she would feel a glimmer of hope that they might make it through the night. However, it was short-lived when Terry placed the last piece of their wood on the fire minutes later.

"That does it, we're out of wood now."

Olivia knew before she touched her clothes that they would still be damp, but prayed she would be wrong. She wasn't. She sighed and put them back on. "I'll go and collect more. There was a large dead tree on the beach that should be dry. I'll work on bringing some of that back. You two warm up a little longer and then try to scavenge around camp a bit to keep the fire going."

"Are you sure? The storm is coming fast and who knows what's out there," Henry said.

Olivia nodded. "Yeah. We need larger branches to keep the fire going all night, and I didn't see much around here. I'll be okay, don't worry," she reassured the others.

She emptied the contents of her backpack in a pile on the ground and selected some clothing: a sweater, wool socks, and a pair of quick-dry pants. After wringing them out and placing them by the fire to dry, she picked up a hatchet and attached it to her belt. She threw the empty backpack on and turned to face Henry and Terry.

"Be careful," Henry said.

"Yeah, be careful. And if you see Owen and Lee, make sure they know they're welcome here. That kid couldn't make a campfire with a blowtorch. As pissed as I am at him, I'd hate to see him and Lee die of hypothermia," Terry said.

"I'll be careful, don't worry," she said before heading out. As she made her way back toward the lake, following the same game trail that led them there, a sense of unease crept back over her. The clouds from the storm had completely overtaken the sun, leaving an eerie darkness lingering in the woods. She could tell the wind was beginning to pick up as the tops of the towering trees scraped together. The rain had started to come down as well, bringing a familiar scent with it. It was just a light sprinkle at this point, but she assumed it was just the beginning.

Olivia's heart raced from the brisk pace she set as she approached the shore of the lake. The waves were much larger than earlier, each towering a foot or two high. If they had crashed in this water, she wouldn't have made it. The mere though filled her with dread. But dwelling on it wouldn't help, so she pressed on toward the downed tree.

When the tree was alive, it would have towered well above its surroundings. Its branches reached the entire distance from brush to water across the rocky shoreline. It had been like this for years though. Its needles were long gone, and its branches had faded white.

As Olivia approached, she unclipped the hatchet from its holster and began chopping at one of the smaller branches, slowly dissecting it. Despite the howling wind, she could hear each crack of the hatchet echo off the surrounding mountains.

She worked efficiently, the sharp blade of the hatchet biting deep into the wood with each swing. Before long, she had amassed a respectable pile of branches. *That's about all I can carry, but with my pack, I should be able to double that amount.*

As she continued to chop, she was startled by a familiar voice behind her. "Hey!"

Olivia's arm froze mid-swing, and she spun around to see who it was. It was Owen, shivering from the cold, with Lee standing behind him. "Oh," Olivia gasped.

"I wasn't expecting to see anyone out here. Just give me a moment to compose myself."

Owen and Lee remained stoic despite Olivia's startle, their bodies pale and shivering, water dripping off their clothes as they stood. She could sense their desperation.

"Are you two okay?"

"Not really," Lee replied, his voice trembling. "Do you have a fire? Maybe a shelter?"

"Yeah, just getting some firewood now. You two look terrible. Come join us."

"Please. I'm so cold," Lee said through his chattering teeth.

"Lee, take a handful of firewood and walk down the beach until you see the game trail about twenty yards down. Follow that until you see the fire. You can't miss it. Go warm up. We won't be too far away," Olivia instructed, pointing Lee in the right direction.

He nodded, grabbed the wood, and stumbled off toward the shelter. Olivia watched him disappear in the thick foliage surrounding the lake before turning to Owen.

"What about you?" she asked. "Are you joining?"

"Sure, I'll come. Terry's going to have a field day with this one, but I can't get a fire going. As much as I hate to admit it, I'll swallow my pride and take his abuse to get warm and dry. Nothing new about that. I get it all the time. Honestly, I don't think I'd survive the night otherwise."

Olivia took another look at Owen. He appeared soaked to his core as rain slicked off his body. His teeth continued chattering and his feet wouldn't stop shaking. "Here, take this and chop some wood. That'll help your body warm up," she said as she handed him the hatchet handle. As he took his first swing, the rain transitioned into an outright downpour.

Owen continued to swing the hatchet at the fallen tree, breaking off large branches as Olivia added them to the pile. As they worked, she saw an opportunity to gather some inside information about the plane crash. "Owen, can I ask you something?"

He stopped swinging, wiped the rain from his eyes, and looked at her, confused. "Sure, what do you want to ask?"

"What happened up there? In the plane."

He hesitated for a moment before responding, "Oh, that. We made a mistake. I grabbed the wrong newspaper this morning, and we didn't know about this storm."

Olivia paused, sensing there was more to the story. "Go on."

He collected himself and exhaled deeply. "We tried to fly around the storm, but it was too big. We tried the radio, but no one responded. It was becoming dangerous, so we decided to make an emergency landing. I have a general knowledge of this area, and there's a huge tundra in the direction we were headed. We're not far away really, but Terry said it was too far to reach, so we ended up landing here, on the lake."

As Olivia processed Owen's words, he continued, "Terry and I have been in this situation a few times before. Storms can move quickly in these parts, you know."

She was shocked. "Wait, this has happened before?"

"Yeah, we've had to land the plane and wait out storms before, but this time was different. As we touched down, something caused the plane to shift, and we lost our landing floats. Craziest thing I've ever seen. Then jumping out of that plane and into that cold lake…that was rough," Owen said, brushing the wet hair, once covered by a hat, out of his face. Olivia presumed he lost the hat in the crash but never asked. "But I'm pretty sure I saw Terry grab his satellite phone. That means once the storm passes, we'll be able to call for help and get out of here."

Owen returned to chopping wood while Olivia mulled over what he had told her. The reality of spending the night in the Alaskan wilderness hit her hard. Despite her experience, the darkness of the night added a whole new level of danger. Large predators roamed the area, and even though she had encountered them before, it would be a lot more unnerving at night. She knew Henry and the others were likely just as scared. *The fire will help. It'll be okay.*

"Let's hope that satellite phone works," Owen said as he handed her the hatchet back.

As Olivia glanced down at the pile of wood, she realized it was too much for them to carry. She loaded her backpack with as many sticks and logs as she could, hoisted it over her shoulders, then grabbed another armful and said, "Let's head back to camp and get warm."

"Can't wait. Hopefully, Terry isn't too hard on me," Owen said as he grabbed a large pile of wood himself and the two of them set off toward the shelter.

# 12

Olivia and Owen retraced their steps to the rock formation, where they found a clothed Lee and Henry huddled around the crackling fire as Terry added a few larger logs to it. The logs burst into flames, emanating a noticeable warmth as Olivia approached. The surrounding rocks acted as natural barriers, preserving the heat and shielding the shelter from the descending temperatures.

Olivia set her pile down on the stack and checked on the clothes she had laid out earlier. They had dried, so she changed into them and placed the soaking clothes she was wearing in their spot. Before she took a seat next to Henry, she watched as Owen lingered on the outskirts of camp.

Knowing the tension between him and Terry, she called out, "Owen, join us by the fire. It's cold and raining out there, and we could use all the warmth we can get."

Owen hesitated for a moment and turned to Terry, who met him with a slight scowl. "Ahh, look who's crawling back."

Owen lowered his head as he made his way to the opposite side of the fire from Terry and sat down. He stripped his clothes off and revealed the state of his body. His hands and feet were blue, and goosebumps covered his skin. He wrung his clothes out before placing them beside the flames to dry.

Owen's appearance didn't stop Terry, as he confronted him with a sharp tone. "Lee mentioned you aren't skilled enough to get a fire going and that he would have died if he hadn't heard Olivia chopping wood. You tried to kill a guest? What's wrong with you?"

Owen acknowledged his words with a subtle nod, but he kept his eyes fixed on the fire. Terry continued taunting Owen's outdoor skills but received no response. Eventually, Terry grew bored and went back to tending the fire with a stick.

Sensing the awkward tension, she changed the subject. "Did the satellite phone work? Are you able to make a call?"

"No. I turned it on when you were out, but I think the storm is blocking the signal. Once it passes, it shouldn't be an issue. I'll make the call then."

"Owen also mentioned that you've dealt with this type of situation before?" This question caused both Henry and Lee to perk up.

"Sounds like you two had quite the chat," Terry said as he glared at Owen.

Olivia noticed Terry seemed nervous by the question and got the impression maybe Owen had shared a few too many details. Terry continued, "A time or two, yeah, but it's been years since I had to land in the remote bush. That was when we were young, dumb, and new to the flying gig. Nowadays, we scout ahead and know what the weather patterns look like. If there's going to be a bad storm like this, we fly around it. It may take an extra hour or two, but it beats spending the night out here." Terry's eyes stayed locked in on Owen as he spoke. Owen never looked up to acknowledge it though.

"So, you're saying this isn't the first time you've sunk a plane?" Henry questioned with amazement, his head tilted.

Terry glared at Henry. "No, this is a first. I've had to land suddenly a time or two, but I've never sunk a plane. Shouldn't have sunk this one either. The plane jerked on me right when it touched down," Terry said, demonstrating how the events unfolded with his hands.

Olivia replayed that moment in her head. It was the sudden jerking that had forced them to make their unexpected layover in this remote wilderness. As a result, she was now stuck here, unable to be with her loved ones back in Montana who were undoubtedly worried sick about her disappearance. Instead, she found herself stranded with a mysterious man, Henry, and two pilots who clearly had a fractured relationship.

"Was it turbulence that jerked the plane?"

"Must have been," Owen said before Terry had a chance to respond. This marked the first time he had spoken since arriving at camp. "Or maybe Terry had a geriatric moment and his hands slipped," he sneered.

Terry gave Owen a sinister death glare. This was enough to shut Owen up, and he retreated to gaze at the fire.

"Must have been a turbulence pocket. I can't really think of anything else," Terry said.

Olivia hadn't heard Lee say much so far, so it startled her when he spoke up and asked, "Once you make that phone call, how long until someone can get us out of here? I have other places I'd prefer to be."

Terry let out a heavy sigh while rolling his eyes. He removed his hat and ran his fingers through his greasy hair. "Sorry for the inconvenience, Lee," he jabbed. "You should be back to your business tomorrow. I'd imagine rescue is just an hour or so away once I make the call."

Lee appeared unfazed by Terry's apparent lack of respect. He nodded his head and muttered under his breath, "The sooner, the better." Olivia felt the same way.

"What if the phone doesn't work? How long until they come looking for us?" Olivia asked.

"I'm afraid rescue would never find us without making contact. We flew hundreds of miles off course trying to avoid the storm," Terry said as he placed another log on the fire. "Don't worry though. This phone works and I charged it overnight, so it's just a matter of getting service."

"I hope so," Olivia said.

"Do you have any idea how they're going to rescue us? Will it be a plane or a helicopter? And what about your plane? Do you think they'll be able to save it?" Henry paused for a moment, seemingly to give his flushed cheeks a moment to relax. "Sorry, I tend to ask too many questions when I get nervous."

Terry didn't appear to mind this line of questioning and answered with a smile. "They'll definitely send a plane out to us. Most planes up here have floats so they can land on rivers or lakes like this one. They wouldn't be confident they would find a suitable place to land a helicopter out here. From what I saw, they wouldn't either. Plus, planes are far more common around here than helicopters."

Henry nodded, appearing to be satisfied with Terry's answer but continued looking at him, as if urging him to continue.

Terry indulged as he said, "As for my plane, I'll leave it. Nobody is going to spend the time or money to recover that thing. It's not worth it. So, it'd be up to me to front the bill and I don't care enough about it to do that. There's nothing in there that's valuable enough for me. Plus, that's what insurance is for, am I right?"

"What kind of deductible do you have to pay for a sunken plane?" Henry asked.

Olivia lost interest in the conversation and tuned it out while she stared at the fire. She thought about her family, about her father. He had lost his mother. He had to be in so much pain right now. Luckily, her mother was there with him, but she desperately wanted to be there as well. To grieve and celebrate the life of her grandma. But due to a sudden jerking of the plane, she was stuck here, waiting for Terry to make a phone call.

As they finished their conversation, Henry turned to Owen and inquired, "What do you think happened? Why'd the plane crash?"

Owen shrugged. "Whatever Terry thinks, I guess." He shifted his focus back to the fire.

Olivia took note that Henry had given up on the conversation and sat in a similar pose to everyone else, gazing at the fire. She looked past their boulder camp and out into the woods. The rock overhang had provided a great shelter because she had completely forgotten about the storm until now. Dark clouds loomed overhead. The rain had transitioned to snow, and lots of it, as it accumulated on the nearby trees.

Henry leaned over to her. "Olivia, while you were gathering firewood, we collected a bit of spruce needles. Figured once they dried out a bit, they would make a halfway decent bed."

"Bed? I have no idea what time it is, but I could get into that idea. Thank you, Henry," she said, now noticing the large pile next to the stacked wood. She walked over to it while Henry and Terry followed her lead. The three of them spread the needles across the few flat areas surrounding the fire.

She grabbed her clothes that had dried next to the fire, balled them together, and placed them down as a makeshift pillow before lying down.

She glanced over at Henry. "I think it's time to call it a night."

"I couldn't agree more. Do you mind if I find a spot next to you?"

"Yeah, that's fine. Looks like there's plenty of room for us both."

"I'm calling it a night too." Terry said as he settled into a spot a few feet away.

"Good night, Terry."

Olivia was exhausted. Although it wasn't night yet, the dark storm clouds gave off that impression. She shifted around before she found a semi-comfortable position. Owen and Lee were still sitting by the fire. "Good night," she called out to them.

The men nodded back in acknowledgment before returning their gaze to the fire.

As she lay her head on the makeshift pillow, her mind wandered once more, back to the events of the day and her plans to return home. She was supposed to check in with her family when she arrived in Seattle. That wasn't happening. She felt awful. They were already dealing with so much, and she didn't need to add to their stress. *Why did I get on that tiny plane?* She knew deep down she should have flown commercial, but Brian made it sound so easy.

Eventually, the exhaustion of the day caught up with her, and she drifted off into a deep, dreamless sleep.

# 13

The glow of the sun rising over the mountain warmed Olivia's face, and she slowly woke up. Her breath was visible as she checked out the campsite and noticed Henry and Owen were still asleep. She rubbed her arms together as she took a second pass but still no sign of Lee or Terry, so she decided to wake the others up. She nudged Henry first, but he resisted and rolled over with a loud groan. She tapped Owen's shoulder and he sprung to his feet.

He rubbed the sleep from his eyes and wrapped his arms around himself to ward off the morning chill. "Good morning. How'd you sleep through that storm?"

Olivia peered beyond the camp and into the trees, where she spotted a blanket of white, powdery snow covering everything. To her surprise, there were only three to four inches, which was much less than the one or two feet she expected to see.

"I slept surprisingly well. I haven't slept that well in years. I guess I didn't realize how tired I was."

"Adrenaline can really drain you," Owen said.

Henry yawned and nodded in agreement. He sat up and stretched his arms. "Do either of you know where the others are?"

Olivia scanned her surroundings. Still no sign of Terry or Lee. She was starting to feel uneasy, but before she could think more about it, she heard a familiar voice echoing from the trees.

"I'm right here," Lee announced as he emerged, holding a small stack of leaves. He gestured to the rest of the group and offered the remaining vegetation to anyone interested in using it as toilet paper.

Henry stood up and walked out of the rock structure, taking the leaves from Lee as he ventured out into the brush. Just as he was almost out of sight, he called out, "I'll be back soon. Don't get rescued without me!"

Olivia made her way to the campfire and put her hands close to the coals, which were still warm. She grabbed the same stick Terry had been using and gathered the coals into a pile, adding some smaller sticks on top of them. Kneeling, she blew air into the embers. They glowed bright red for a moment before fading. Olivia blew on the coals once more and the sticks ignited.

She relished the warmth from the crackling flames, carefully adding larger logs from the dwindling woodpile as the fire consumed the smaller pieces. It was evident that someone, likely Terry, had been tending to the fire throughout the night. As she touched the surrounding rocks, she felt the gradual release of the heat they had absorbed during those hours. It was clear how she had experienced such restful sleep—the comforting warmth surrounding the campsite had played a significant role.

She remembered weekends spent at her grandma's house: the wood stove in the living room, its comforting heat, the crackling timber, and the familiar scent. What she wouldn't give to be back there now.

"Lee, did you happen to see Terry out there gathering wood?" she asked.

"No, I didn't see him. Do you want me to gather some wood though?"

Olivia glanced over at the woodpile. "Yes, please, that would be great. We only have a few logs left."

Lee nodded as he walked back to the fire and sat in the same spot as the night prior. "Let me warm up for a minute. It's cold," he said as he rubbed his hands together over the flames.

Olivia took a closer look at Lee as he warmed up. His tie had gone missing, and his suit jacket was torn in multiple places. He didn't come across as the outdoorsy type and she wondered how he was faring, but before she could ask, Owen spoke up.

"Hey Olivia, do you mind if I borrow that hatchet? I'll go get some wood now."

"Sure, go ahead," she replied, handing it over. "And while you're out there, keep an eye out for Terry too. He should have been back by now, right?"

"Who knows? Terry does whatever Terry wants to do. I wouldn't worry too much. He'll show up," Owen said nonchalantly and headed away from camp.

Rising to his feet, Lee said, "I'll go help Owen."

"Sounds good."

Olivia collected the contents from her bag, which remained scattered next to her bedding and carried them closer to the fire. While sorting through it all, Henry came back and sat next to her, warming himself by the fire.

"Did you by chance happen to find any cinnamon rolls in there?"

Olivia chuckled. "Afraid not, but I wish I did. Did you happen to spot Terry out there?"

"Nope," Henry sighed, shaking his head. "I saw loads of footprints in the snow, but I haven't seen him since last night."

"I'm guessing he went up the mountain to try to get a signal. It's just strange that he didn't let anyone know."

Henry nodded and paused for a second. "That's probably right, but that doesn't seem strange to me at all. Despite being chatty at times, I think Terry is somewhat of a hermit. With Owen getting on his nerves yesterday, some alone time might do him good." Henry leaned forward and peeked into her bag. "If there are no cinnamon rolls, do you have any doughnuts instead? I'm partial to the ones with sprinkles, but I'll settle for a glazed one in a pinch," Henry said, ending with a laugh.

Olivia laughed as well and continued to rummage through her possessions. "No doughnuts I'm afraid, but I do have another treat."

She quickly inspected her floral mug, relieved to find no cracks. With a smile, she reached for a black fleece coat and another pair of socks. She wrapped them around the mug before setting it beside the fire. Afterward, she grabbed a handful of granola bars and placed them next to her. She gestured to Henry not to touch them, explaining they were for the entire group. But in a hushed tone, she whispered, "I do have something we can share as long as you promise to keep it a secret."

She picked up a small bag of gummy bears and handed it to him. His face beamed with excitement as he struggled to yank it open from both sides, but it didn't budge. Olivia smiled and pointed out the tear line.

"Ohh, it's one of those," Henry noted, his face flushed but still smiling. He tore the bag open along the perforated line and handed it back to Olivia. She grabbed a few of the brightly colored gummy bears and passed the bag back. With a cheesy grin, he asked, "How'd you know to pack my favorite snack of all time?"

"I always try to make sure my guests are well taken care of. The options were limited at the lodge store though. I may have gone through every bag of Skittles that came into that place this year, but I'm not ashamed." Olivia grinned as she devoured the gummy bears.

The two of them chuckled together as they finished the entire bag of candy and then burned the evidence in the campfire. Moments later, Lee and

Owen arrived with a load of firewood, and they instantly noticed the pile of granola bars. Owen couldn't hold back from squealing, "You have food! That's fantastic! Wait, please tell me you're sharing it with all of us?"

"Of course, what's mine is ours. We're all in this together. However, if I had any doughnuts or gummy bears, that might be a different story," Olivia said with a wink to Henry. He struggled to stifle his laughter, so he averted his eyes from the others.

"Very nice of you, Olivia. Can we split a couple of those up now? I'm starving," Owen said.

Olivia agreed and unwrapped two bars, tossing the trash into the nearby flames. The wrappers instantly incinerated as she snapped each bar in half and handed the others each a piece.

With food in hand, Olivia approached the others and raised a toast before taking a bite.

"Are these huckleberries?" Henry asked.

"I believe so, nice touch," she responded.

As she took another bite, Henry corrected himself, "No, these are blackberries. Tasty but not quite as good as a huckleberry."

"What's a huckleberry?" Owen asked.

"It doesn't matter," Lee interrupted, "that's what it is. Thanks, Olivia, I appreciate it."

Olivia nodded. After finishing up her snack, she went back to her pile of items. She grabbed a headlamp and pushed the button to turn it on, but it didn't do anything. "Dead," she said disappointedly and set it aside.

She unzipped a small tan bag with a fly-fishing fly pattern on it, revealing a fly box, some spools of tippet, nippers, and a bottle of fly floatant. Satisfied that everything was in order, she zipped it back up. Then, she grabbed a red bandanna and uncovered her fly reel. She spun the reel around, checking that it was still in working order.

"It appears you're missing a rod," Henry said.

Olivia placed the rod on the ground and folded her arms. "It was in the side pocket of the pack, but it must have fallen out during the chaos. It looks like it has a new home at the bottom of the lake." Olivia paused for a moment as the revelation sunk in. "That rod was a gift, you know. One of the only things James ever gave me. It meant a lot to me."

"Who's James?" Henry inquired.

"My late fiancé," Olivia said as her eyes betrayed a mix of emotions that she tried to hide.

"Oh. You've never mentioned him before. Is there a story with the rod?" Henry probed.

"Well, it wasn't so much a gift as it was an 'I'm sorry, please forgive me' present." Olivia chuckled to herself before continuing.

"We were on our first backpacking trip, which I had just found out was also his first. Can you believe the man couldn't figure out how to set up a tent? It cracks me up every time I think of it, especially now, looking back at how much camping we ended up doing. Anyway, he said he would break down and pack up our fishing stuff while I set the tent up. Typically, that means putting the rod back into the rod tube, but apparently, not to him. I didn't find that out until we made it back home the next day and I was organizing my camping stuff. I went to check on my rod, unzipped the tube, and it was empty.

"Well, I called him and asked what happened and he froze. 'I'm so sorry, Olivia, I'll make it up to you, I promise.' It was just a cheapo rod, so I didn't really mind, but he came over the next day with that bad boy. It was a Winston. They make very nice rods, and I caught a ton of fish on that thing over the years. I'm sad to see it go. It was one of the few things I had left of him." A tear fell down her cheek. She quickly wiped it away, took a deep breath, and put a smile on.

"I'm sorry, Olivia. I know that's tough. Do you want to talk more about him?" Henry comforted her, resting a hand on her shoulder.

"Thanks, Henry. Maybe another time." She dug back into her pile and brought out the final items: a water purification device, an empty water bottle, and a full water bottle.

Opening it up, she took a sip. She hadn't realized how thirsty she was until that point, but she felt her body instantly refreshed. She took another drink before realizing no one else had had any water either, so she offered the bottle to the others. "Does anyone need a drink?" Everyone's hand raised, so she passed the bottle around.

Henry glanced at the stack of firewood. "Looks like you two brought back a lot of wood. Thankfully, it's starting to warm up though. Once Terry comes back from that call, I don't think we'll need any of it, but still, thanks!"

Olivia noticed that much of the snow had already melted away from the trees, and the snow on the ground was nearly gone as well. When she turned to Henry, she saw his mouth sunken in a frown. "How are you holding up, Henry?"

"I'm okay. I was just thinking about my wife. She must be worried sick. We were supposed to go out to our favorite restaurant tonight and catch an opera. Guess that won't be happening."

"I'm sorry. You can call her tonight and tell her you'll be back tomorrow. She won't have to worry long," Olivia said, placing her hand on his shoulder.

"I know, I know. My son would have loved it here though. He used to come on these fishing trips with me back in the day, but not anymore. Too busy with work. I'm sure it'll take him weeks before he realizes…if I never make it back."

"I'm sure he cares. He's probably as torn up about this as the rest of your family."

Henry nodded but didn't respond.

"So, I guess we're just sitting here and waiting for Terry to come back, right?" Lee said.

"I suppose so," Owen said.

Olivia shifted, chewing on her conversation with Henry, reminding her of her favorite date with James.

***

It was the coldest day of the year. The bone-chilling cold intertwined with the frustration of her car's refusal to start. Whining and grinding, it added an unexpected layer of stress to the test she was late for. She urgently called James for a ride to campus.

"James, are you awake?"

"I sure am. I'm actually on my way to campus to talk to my advisor. What's up?"

"Can you please pick me up? My car won't start."

"You bet. I'll be there in ten."

Peering anxiously through her front door, Olivia spotted James's black F-150 pulling up. She hurried out and hopped into the front seat.

She kissed him and said, "Thank you so much. You're a lifesaver. I can't miss this test."

"Of course!" James placed his hand on her leg, and she felt her heart rate increase at his touch. "Hey, if your car won't start, that means you're stranded today, right?"

"Theoretically, yeah. I can find a ride home from campus though."

"What about dinner? Can I cook you something?"

Olivia hesitated. They had been dating for over a year, and he had yet to cook for her.

"You want to make me dinner? Should I be worried?"

James stopped at a stop sign and shot her a puzzled look. "What does that mean? I'm a great cook."

She smirked. "Sure. I'll be home at five. Come over any time after that."

That evening, Olivia was sitting at her kitchen table finishing an assignment when she heard the doorbell ring.

"Come in!" she called out.

James stumbled through the door, grappling with a large, brown carryout bag that immediately caught Olivia's attention.

"James, did you get carryout?" she asked, her voice soft as she wrapped her arms around him. "I thought you were cooking?"

James leaned in, his lips brushing gently against hers. "I did say that, huh? I wanted to. I really did. Turns out I don't actually know how to cook. I called my mom to see if she'd walk me through some stuff, but she was busy. I bought steak instead."

Olivia chuckled as she grabbed silverware and plates from the kitchen, setting them on the table while James took out two boxed meals and a candlestick. He pulled a lighter from his pocket and lit the candle.

"What's up, James? What's with all the theatrics?"

"Am I that obvious?"

"Yeah."

James slowly dropped down to one knee and reached out for Olivia's hand. She gasped softly, feeling the warmth of his touch as he tightly caressed her hand, his thumb tracing gentle circles against her skin.

"Olivia, growing up, I never thought I would be the type to settle down and get married. I feared it would lead to a life of monotony, turning me into a fat slug like my parents' marriage seemed to be. But everything changed when I met you. Every day you bring excitement into my life. We fell in love adventuring and pushing each other out of our comfort zones. No part of my being believes I would ever live a monotonous life with you. Exactly the contrary. I can't imagine living life without you."

Olivia's face turned bright red and her stomach fluttered. Before she could respond, he took out a small box from his jacket pocket.

"Olivia, I want to spend the rest of my life with you. Will you marry me?" James's voice trembled as he opened the small box, revealing a small but elegant ring.

Is this really happening?

Olivia dropped down to her knees, her eyes glistening with tears of happiness.

"Yes."

***

# 14

"Still no sign of Terry after all these hours," Henry said, breaking the tense silence that lingered around camp. "Should we go search for him?" With a shaky voice, he looked toward Olivia for guidance.

Olivia's mind churned as she thought more about Terry's disappearance. If he had left to make a call, surely he would be back by now. Unless maybe something had gone wrong. He had the satellite phone, their only means of communication with the outside world. Without it, their chances of rescue were nonexistent. They needed Terry.

Lee and Owen had both fallen asleep and were starting to wake up. As they rubbed their eyes, she mirrored Henry's sentiment.

"I think we need to go search for Terry," she said, her eyes darting between the others. "He should be back by now. The terrain is treacherous—unstable rocks, fallen trees, and dense vegetation. It's easy to get disoriented in this kind of landscape. Or worse, he could have fallen and broken something."

Owen let out a big yawn. "You're right. I nearly rolled my ankle three times while collecting wood this morning. Terry's in terrible shape too. I'm surprised he made it back to the lake, let alone any farther without getting hurt somehow. I can't believe I didn't think of that earlier."

Lee, now hovering over the fire, chimed in, "That sounds like a plan to me. We need to find Terry and, most importantly, that satellite phone. I've been away long enough."

Henry nodded in agreement. "Count me in. I'd prefer not to spend another night here if possible."

"Let's do it then. I was thinking the best approach would be to split into two groups and check the two surrounding peaks. If Terry didn't get any service here, I imagine that's where he would have the best chance," Olivia concluded.

Owen stood next to Lee, his arms crossed and his left foot tapping. "That's a great plan," he said. He turned to Lee, asking, "How about joining me toward the eastern peak?"

Lee hesitated a moment as his eyes darted toward Olivia, but eventually nodded and replied with a simple, "Sure."

"That leaves the western peak for us," Henry said.

Olivia was relieved with how the pairings turned out but tried her best not to show it. There was something about Lee that unsettled her. He seemed flat, emotionless, and mostly just inconvenienced by the situation. It was odd.

Owen, on the other hand, seemed like a whole new person without Terry around. He was more engaged, confident, and friendly. She would have been okay pairing with him, but she trusted Henry. He saved her life, and she was certain he'd do it again if it came to that.

"Perfect, let's go to the lake. I have this water purification system that we can use to refill the bottles. If these mountains are anything like the ones back home, we'll need as much water as we can get," Olivia said.

"Agreed," Owen exclaimed. "But let's clean up first. Does anyone have any food other than Olivia? Please put everything in the backpack; we need to hang it up. I don't want to come back to a hungry bear eating everything."

"I wish," Henry said. Lee shook his head, indicating he didn't have anything either.

"I don't see Terry's bag anywhere, so just these bars… Bummer," Owen said as he placed them in the bag. He took off one of his bracelets before asking to borrow Olivia's knife. "Paracord bracelet. I saw them at a gift shop once and thought, 'Why not? This will come in handy one day.' Sure enough, today's that day."

Owen cut the bracelet and slowly began to unravel it, revealing one long strand of paracord. He tied one end to a rock and walked away from camp and over to a large overhanging branch. He attempted to toss it over the branch, but he botched it badly. After watching a few more failed attempts, Olivia grabbed her backpack and walked over to him.

"Can I try?" she asked, reaching her hand out for the rock.

Owen looked down at her hand and then up to her eyes. His face lacked emotion. "One more try. I've got it dialed in. This is the one." He threw the rock one more time, but he didn't have it dialed in. The rock flew two feet under the branch before crashing into the brush. "Here, it's not as easy as it looks."

Olivia reached over for the paracord, holding back a smile. She reeled in the rock and ensured the cordage was still tightly secured. The rock was about the size of a softball, something she had held many times in her college rec leagues. She gripped it tight, wound her arm up, and let it fly. The rock soared through the air, easily passing over the branch before crashing down.

"Lucky toss," Owen muttered as he retrieved the rock.

Olivia couldn't hide her smile any longer but refrained from saying anything. She'd set hundreds of bear lines growing up, and having been the pitcher on her rec league team, she knew her way around a softball. There was no luck about it.

Once Owen returned with the rock, he untied the paracord and secured it to the backpack. Olivia then pulled down on the rope, causing the bag to fly up into the air. Once it was hanging a few inches below the branch, she tied off the end around the tree. The bear line was now set, and they had peace of mind knowing their food would be safe while they searched for Terry.

As the two walked back to camp, Owen muttered, "Thanks for the help."

She could sense the resentment in his voice, but she didn't let it bother her. She had dealt with fragile egos before and knew exactly how to handle them. "Of course. Let me know the next time you need any help. I'd be more than willing to assist."

Owen's eyes narrowed on her as his brows furrowed. He quickly looked away and changed the subject. "So, about that water? Let's get going. I don't want to hike in the dark."

"I'm ready," Lee said and followed Owen out of camp and toward the lake.

Once the two were out of sight, Henry leaned over to Olivia, ensuring only she could hear. "I'm so happy I got paired with you. There's just something off about those two."

Olivia handed Henry the empty water bottles and grabbed her water filter before whispering back, "I know, I'm getting that feeling too. Let's get going though."

# 15

As Olivia and Henry approached the lake shore, Lee and Owen were looking down at a large, warped, white piece of metal. As she walked closer, she realized what it was: plane wreckage. The rocky beach was scattered with metal debris, a haunting reminder of the wreck they survived.

"Wow, we all really made it out of this crash," Olivia said.

Owen put his arm around her shoulder, brought her in tight, and said, "That's because we're survivors, and that's what we'll continue to do: survive."

Although Olivia appreciated the sentiment, she couldn't shake the uneasiness she felt around Owen now that Henry had mentioned it. Initially relieved by his newfound persona without Terry, she grew increasingly unsettled. There was something off about him, and she couldn't quite put her finger on it. She subtly shifted away from his embrace and took a few steps away to create some distance between them.

He didn't appear to notice and started to gather pieces of sheet metal, stacking them in a pile. Lee and Henry followed his lead while Olivia went to the shore to fill up the water bottles. She placed one end of the filter's hose into the water, the other into one of the water bottles, and pumped.

While she did, she scanned the lake, taking in the rugged beauty of the landscape. Besides debris scattering the beach, the lake itself was a breathtaking sight. Its crystal-clear waters shimmered in the sunlight, reflecting the towering peaks. The mountains rose majestically on each side, their snowcapped summits reaching toward the clear blue sky.

Olivia's eyes traced the outlines of the two gigantic peaks, which seemed to touch the heavens. They were steep and foreboding, challenging even for experienced climbers. *No way Terry would have made it to the top of either one.* She shifted her gaze down to examine the sides of the mountains.

Amid their rocky face, Olivia noticed a few knobs on each mountain that protruded less sharply from the terrain. They seemed slightly more manageable and potentially accessible for someone looking to signal for help. *That's where I would have gone.*

"I really thought Terry would have returned by now," Olivia announced to the others while she finished filling the last of her water bottles and sealed their lids tight.

"It's okay, Olivia. I know Terry has the satellite phone and a lifetime of experience, but I'll make sure we'll make it out of here alive," Owen declared, walking over toward her to retrieve a water bottle.

She handed it to him and reluctantly said, "Oh, thanks, Owen. I'm so glad you're here. I'm not sure what we'd do without you." She wanted to add in the fact that he and Lee almost froze to death the night before, and that it was Terry's pack and her skills that kept them dry and warm throughout the night. Instead, she just handed him the bottle with a sideways smile, keeping her reservations to herself.

Owen reciprocated the smile, oblivious to her inner monologue, and took the opportunity to assert more of his leadership. "Let's be sure to be back before dusk. We should avoid hiking in the dark and making it any more challenging than it already is."

"Agreed. Stay safe and see you soon," Henry responded softly. Olivia nodded in agreement, maintaining her pleasant facade.

Owen made his way over to Lee, indicating his readiness, before turning back to address the others once more, saying, "Stay safe and be loud. The wilderness in Alaska is unforgiving."

"You too," Olivia said, watching as they departed into the distance.

When they found themselves alone on the shore, Olivia turned to Henry. "Well then, what would we do without that man's guidance?"

Henry laughed. "He did sound a tad arrogant there, didn't he?"

"For sure," she replied with a chuckle. "Well, let's get going. I saw a few knobs that I think Terry would have tried to get up to. Let's see if we can find any sign of him there."

Once the two had maneuvered into the trees and started to make their way up toward the ridge, Henry said, "I know Owen's kind of out there, but I have a really bad feeling about Lee."

Olivia's instincts aligned with his. "I have the same feeling," she responded. "He doesn't speak much, does he? And what was with him on the plane? It seemed like he made a deliberate effort to be the first one out, without any regard for us. He had to have seen you stuck, but instead of helping, he just bailed."

"I saw that," Henry said. "He's also very guarded. It's so hard to tell what he's thinking, and I have no idea why he's out here. He seems like a typical city person, not an outdoorsman or anyone else you'd imagine meeting in a town like King Salmon."

Olivia paused to consider. She faintly remembered Brian talking about some mining company from Washington state that wanted to build twenty or so miles away from the fishing lodge. He had been outraged by the idea and had called in every favor he could to try and stop it. Before she could share that with Henry, he spoke up.

"I've heard rumors that there was a proposal to build a massive mine in that area a few months ago, but I thought it was rejected. I wonder if he's involved in that."

Olivia bit her lip, adding, "I heard the same thing from Brian. He definitely has the look of a businessman. He is wearing a suit after all. Well, what's left of one."

"I'd guess he was involved in that. Maybe a lawyer or executive coming back to restart the conversation."

"He seems the type, that's for sure. I just can't shake the feeling there's more to him than meets the eye."

# 16

Olivia and Henry continued into the brush and toward the ridge, following a small game trail until they reached a fork. "Which direction should we take?" Henry asked.

Olivia took a moment to survey the area. The trees were tall and the canopy thick, making it hard to see more than a few yards in any direction. She continued to evaluate the area until finally making out pieces of the rocky slope in the distance. After being certain her eyes weren't deceiving her, she pointed it out to Henry and confidently said, "That's where we need to be. I think the left path gets us there."

To ensure they could easily find their way back, she removed her hatchet out of its case, and walked over to a small cedar tree. She grasped a branch and, with one swing of the hatchet, cut it off. She repeated this four more times until she had a handful of branches, which she placed on the trail.

"Trail marker," she said as she wiped the sap from her hands on her pant leg. When they return down the trail, she'll know which way to go.

"You're pretty smart. I take it you've spent a lot of time outdoors?"

"I have," she said, trying to avoid sounding boastful. "Growing up in Montana, nature was our playground. Weekends were all about fishing, hiking, camping, you name it. But fishing was always my favorite, and the best spots are often hidden away. My dad taught me this trick to mark the trail. They'll eventually get picked up by the wind or knocked aside by an animal and blend back into nature."

"That's pretty good—leave no trace."

She smiled back at him. "Exactly."

"Hey, I've been meaning to ask you…How did you end up in Alaska? I imagine there are plenty of guiding opportunities down in Montana too."

Olivia's stomach dropped as a wave of emotions washed over her. Memories of past events flooded her mind, and she could feel her nerves tingle.

Henry noticed the sudden change in her demeanor and instinctively crossed his arms. Realizing it, he backtracked. "Oh, I didn't mean to bring up any bad memories. I'm sorry."

"It's okay," she replied, taking a moment to collect her thoughts. "It's a tough story, honestly. It all comes back to my fiancé."

This was the first time Olivia had considered telling this story to anyone in Alaska. Over time, she had grown accustomed to answering questions about why she was there with common lies, like being desperate for adventure or wanting to escape civilization. But the truth was very different, and it hurt too much to talk about. Yet, with Henry, she felt a sense of trust and comfort she hadn't experienced before.

"When James left this world, everything at home and every routine I had became unbearable. I tried to carry on with my normal day-to-day, but everything reminded me of him. I'd find myself sobbing in the grocery store, right in front of the bananas, recalling some silly joke he made there. Or just walking downtown, passing by the store where he first held my hand, and I'd break down. I once had to pull over because I was sobbing uncontrollably when I passed a trailhead we intended on hiking. I was a mess. I couldn't function anymore, so I had to leave," Olivia said, her voice trembling.

Tears streamed down her face. The weight of her loss felt raw as she unearthed it from the depths where she had buried it. She desperately wished for it to dissipate.

Henry took a step forward and embraced her. Olivia let go and sobbed in his arms. He provided a much-needed source of support.

"I'm sorry. I know it's tough, but talking about them is how we remember them. Thank you so much for sharing this with me. I'm always here for you whenever you need me," he said gently, continuing to hold her as she wept.

Olivia felt a sense of understanding and empathy. They exchanged a brief, comforting smile, and she nestled back into his embrace, grateful for his support.

After a while, her tears subsided, and she listened to the noises around them. Birds chirped in the distance, and she could hear two squirrels going back and forth. The rustle of branches caused by small gusts of wind filled the air. She pulled away and wiped the tears with her hand.

With Henry by her side, they continued on their journey, walking side by side in companionable silence, finding solace in each other's presence.

# 17

After a while of trekking through the dense forest, pushing through thick undergrowth and overcoming rugged terrain, Olivia and Henry finally broke out above the tree line and found themselves standing on top of an overlook. The view that greeted them was nothing short of magnificent. The vast expanse of the landscape unfolded before their eyes, revealing a breathtaking panorama. Mountain peak after mountain peak stretched into the distance, each one more rugged and imposing than the last.

Olivia stood still, allowing herself a moment to catch her breath and simply exist among the breathtaking surroundings. The vastness and beauty of nature enveloped her. She unscrewed the cap of her water bottle and took a long, refreshing gulp. She extended the bottle to Henry, who gratefully accepted.

As she regained her breath and her heart rate normalized, she gazed out at the scene below, her eyes drawn to the lake. Its crystal-clear waters reflected the golden hues of the sun. She marveled at its tranquility.

Her attention shifted to the opposing ridgeline. She squinted her eyes, searching for any signs of movement, hoping to catch a glimpse of Owen and Lee. She imagined they would have made it to above the tree line around the same time. She scanned every nook and cranny, every overhang and opening, but her efforts proved fruitless. They were nowhere to be seen.

Turning her attention to the ridge where she was standing, she searched for any signs of Terry. Her eyes darted from rock to rock, bush to bush, and up and down the exposed route. Unfortunately, there was no trace of him. No footprints. No broken twigs. No overturned rock. Nothing.

"I don't see Terry or the others anywhere," Olivia reported.

Henry's forehead creased as he surveyed the setting as well. "I don't see them either. Do you think we should continue up the ridge or turn back? I'd guess we don't have many more hours of daylight left, and we're likely staying here another night. If that's the case, we really need to gather a few more supplies."

Olivia considered Henry's words, weighing their options. The thought of not finding Terry, or the satellite phone, was unsettling. Same with the thought of spending another night out there, especially if they were unprepared.

"Let's head back," she said. "There's no sign of him up here. We should regroup, but I hope they were able to find Terry. If not, we'll need to figure out what to do next."

As they prepared to leave the overlook, Olivia took one final glance at the magnificent scenery surrounding them. She had hiked many mountains in her day and seen just as many alpine lakes, but the pure wilderness and beauty she was surrounded by seemed to outrank everything else at that moment.

"Incredible," she whispered.

"I couldn't say it any better," Henry said.

As they made their way down the ridge, the terrain became increasingly challenging. The path narrowed, and the ground beneath them grew steep and slippery. Henry's foot slipped on a loose patch of gravel, causing him to lose his balance. He instinctively flailed his arms in an attempt to regain stability.

Without hesitation, she lunged forward and grabbed hold of Henry's arm, pulling him back from the edge just as he was about to topple over.

Gasping for breath, Henry looked at her with gratitude and awe. "You…you saved me," he stuttered.

They both took a moment to collect themselves as their heart rates gradually steadied. The near-death experience served as a stark reminder of the dangers that lurked around them despite the beauty. As they continued down the mountain, Olivia reminded herself to move with care, her steps more deliberate and her senses attuned to every potential hazard.

# 18

The hair on the back of Olivia's neck rose as she and Henry returned to camp, noticing the unlit campfire and the bag of food still hanging from the branch.

"It looks like we're the first ones back," Olivia said.

"It does."

Henry called out for Owen and Lee. His voice echoed through the air but was only met with silence.

"I'd hoped they'd be back already," Olivia said. She leaned against a tree, taking a moment to let her heart rate return to normal. As she did, her stomach rumbled. "That hike really took a lot out of me. Are you hungry?" she asked, looking over at Henry with a tired smile.

"Famished." His stomach rumbled in agreement. He absentmindedly checked his wrist, only to realize he wasn't wearing a watch. "I think we've been out for three, maybe four hours," he estimated.

"Sounds about right," Olivia said as she walked over to the hanging bear bag. "The days are so long up here, even in the fall, that it's hard to tell how much time has passed." She untied the bag and lowered it to the ground. She picked out a granola bar and handed it to Henry. "Here, let's share this. I'll get the fire started again."

Henry eagerly took on the task and opened the bar's packaging. He broke it in half, putting Olivia's portion aside, and took a bite while reviewing the wrapper. "Huh, these *are* huckleberries. I could have sworn they were blackberries," he said.

"They're from back home. The last of my stash. Lots of wild huckleberries where I'm from," Olivia shared as she took a break from the fire and enjoyed a bite of the bar. A small grin tugged at the corner of her lips. "We used to hike up to the high country every August with the intention of collecting as many of them as possible. Mom always claimed she made the best huckleberry jelly. I remember gathering bags and bags of them growing up, but we never had any jelly.

They would all be gone by the time we got back home."

"That sounds amazing. I've had huckleberries a few times here and there while traveling, but never fresh from the mountains. I can only imagine how much better they must be."

"So much better. I'll have to wait until next year though. By the time I get back, they'll already be out of season." After she finished off the remainder of what would be her dinner, she directed her attention back to building the fire. She added a few more sticks to her base and, with the strike of a match, she had it burning. *Thank goodness Terry left the matches.* No telling what she would have done without those. As she added a few larger sticks to the fire, she settled down next to Henry.

The crackling fire cast dancing shadows on the rocks around them. The warmth of the flames contrasted with the cool mountain air, and Olivia could feel herself relaxing in its embrace. But even amid this tranquil moment, she couldn't shake the feeling that something was bothering Henry.

The flickering light played on his face, revealing a subtle tension in his jaw. With a gentle touch, she placed her hand on his shoulder, silently letting him know she was there for him. She waited for him to open up, but he remained silent. She finally asked, "How are you doing?"

His gaze remained fixated on the dancing flames, his thoughts distant. "I'm okay."

She moved closer, providing a comforting presence. "You can talk to me, Henry."

His gaze shifted from the fire to Olivia, a mixture of vulnerability and resolve flickering in his eyes. He took a deep breath. "I was thinking about my son."

"What about him?"

"He used to come with me on all these adventures, but we never made it out to Alaska. He's grown and married now, living on the other side of the country. I barely get to see him. I planned this trip as a way to spend some quality time with him, but he couldn't make it."

"I'm sorry to hear that," she offered. "It can be tough watching children grow and watch as life takes them on different paths. So my dad says," she added with a smile.

"That's not all," he said, his voice wavering slightly. "He called me and my wife right before I left and told us they're expecting. I'm going to be a grandpa. And now all I can think about is, what if he had come with me? He could have died in that plane crash. Or what if we don't make it out of here? I would have been the reason that child grows up without a father."

Olivia's eyes widened as she absorbed Henry's words. She gently squeezed his hand, offering support in her touch.

"How many of these do you have left?" Henry asked after a few minutes passed.

Olivia snapped back to the present, checked the bag, and responded, "Two. The others can split one like we did, and I assume Terry will have his own. If they find him, that is."

"I hope so. Otherwise, we'll need to find another way out of here. And much more food. Speaking of food, I could use some more."

That's when Olivia had an idea. She looked up at Henry and said, "How about this, can you grab some more firewood? We're going to need it. While you do that, I'm going to work on a way to get something else to eat."

"Deal," Henry said without hesitation. He snatched Olivia's hatchet and made his way into the depths of the surrounding trees. The flames from the campfire flickered as he disappeared, leaving Olivia to focus on her plan.

# 19

Olivia ventured away from camp on a quest to find the perfect stick. She picked up various contenders one by one, assessing each before casting it aside. Her standards were exact: a stick that was long and slender, devoid of excessive branching, yet sturdy. After considering multiple options, she finally found the ideal specimen—an approximately eight-foot-long stick with a diameter similar to a nickel. Satisfied with her selection, she made her way back to camp.

With her knife in hand, she began the delicate task of whittling the stick down, envisioning its transformation into a fishing rod. Uncertain of the outcome, she knew she had to try. Success would grant her the ability to catch fish. And fish meant food.

It didn't have to be perfect, she reasoned, just functional. A modest tool capable of delivering one-tenth of the effectiveness of a regular fly rod. As she applied careful knife strokes, her confidence in her technique grew, motivating her to shape the wood into a semblance of the fly rod she had wielded countless times before.

Half an hour later, Henry made his way back to camp, carrying a hefty load of wood for the eighth time. Finally catching sight of Olivia's handiwork, he marveled, "That's incredible. It looks like one of those bamboo rods hanging as decoration in fly shops."

Olivia returned a satisfied smile. "Exactly! I'm quite pleased with how it's turning out. Now I just need a way to attach the line to it." She paused for a moment as she tried to think of a solution. "Any suggestions?"

Henry's brow furrowed as he contemplated. "Honestly, I'm drawing a blank."

"Actually, I might have an idea," she said, turning to her bag and pulling out a fly box.

She selected four sizable flies, reminiscing about the time she had purchased the size-eight grasshopper imitations many years ago but had never found an occasion to employ them. They had remained untouched, tucked away in her fly box until this very moment. Now was their time to prove their worth.

With the fly box closed and returned to her bag, she grabbed the first fly and removed all the foam and string until only the bare hook remained. Delicately aligning it against the stick, she positioned it as a guide and pressed the hook firmly into the wood. She manipulated the hook and bent it around the stick, ensuring both ends were firmly anchored. Smiling with pride, she inspected her handiwork. It wasn't perfect by any means, but she knew it would work. She repeated the process for the remaining flies, executing each step with precision and purpose.

"It may not be the prettiest, but I think it'll do the job. Let's give it a try," she announced.

"I think it looks fantastic! It's definitely going to attract fish."

Olivia gathered her reel, fly box, and all the other fishing essentials before setting off with Henry toward the lake. Once they arrived, she began to string the rod.

As Henry watched on, he commented, "It certainly looks the part."

"It won't have the same speed or power as my other rod, but I think it'll work in a pinch."

However, she frowned with concern. "I never thought I'd say this, but I hope I don't hook anything too big. I'm afraid the guides might fall off or the rod might snap in half."

Henry chuckled. "That's not something you ever hear from an angler." He glanced toward her fly box as she sifted through the various options. "So, what flies are you considering?"

Olivia scanned the lake, catching sight of a few fish breaking the surface, leaving behind gentle ripples. As she observed their behavior, she mentally assessed her fly pattern options.

"I'm leaning toward either a classic dry fly, like an Adams or a Wulff, maybe an ant to mimic whatever's making them rise, or perhaps a Woolly Bugger to entice them below the surface. What do you think?"

"There are a few rising, so a dry fly sounds like a good choice, but there's something about a Bugger. They just always seem to catch fish."

Olivia was already tying on a black Woolly Bugger before Henry could finish his sentence. "I agree. I've always had more success with Buggers than dry flies. And this is about catching fish, right? So, let's catch some fish." She swung the homemade pole in the air. "Well, here goes nothing."

Olivia methodically swung the rod back and forth, allowing the line to extend in the air before finally shooting it across the lake's surface. She couldn't help but beam as she watched the fly land on the water. Shifting her focus to the line, she slowly retrieved it. Unexpectedly, she felt a quick jerk on the other end, and with lightning-fast reflexes, she set the hook and signaled she had a fish on the line.

"Fish on!" she yelled, her voice echoing across the lake.

Henry laughed. "Amazing! First cast magic."

Olivia let out an excited laugh as she worked the fish toward the shore. The small fish put up quite the fight, especially against her stiff homemade rod. It was no match for her and her skillful angling though, and she quickly brought it to shore. Once there, she tugged it out of the water and removed the hook. She then placed the small fish on the shore where she knew it couldn't escape.

She handed the rod to Henry with a grin of accomplishment. "You're up," she said.

Olivia pulled out her knife from her pocket, intending to clean the fish.

"Well, you set the bar pretty high there, but I'll give it a go," Henry said.

Olivia watched as he tried to replicate her success. He swung the rod back and forth, gradually loading the fly line before he shot it out toward the water. He slowly retrieved the fly back to shore but wasn't able to sway any fish's attention. He turned to Olivia and jokingly asked, "Any tips, guide?"

She laughed. "You know what you're doing; it just takes time. Not everyone can be as good as I am."

Henry chuckled and continued casting.

Olivia unfolded her knife and made a clean cut down the belly of the fish. This allowed her to remove its innards, preparing it for cooking over a campfire. Satisfied with her work, she walked toward the nearby lake, intending to rinse the fish in the cool, fresh water. But Henry's sudden and exuberant yell startled her.

"Fish on!" he yelled. Olivia watched as he meticulously worked the fish to shore.

"Congratulations. You've got dinner tonight!"

"And I'll definitely be eating it," he said. He placed the fish down on the ground and swapped the rod for Olivia's knife.

As Olivia cast and began her slow retrieval, she instinctively scanned the shoreline until she spotted something moving toward them a few hundred feet away. "Henry, do you see that?" she asked, pointing down the shore.

Henry rose to his feet and looked in the direction she pointed, spotting a small, dark figure approaching.

"Bear," Henry declared.

# 20

"Bear," Olivia repeated as her slow retrieval was interrupted by a small fish striking her fly. "Perfect," she said, reeling the fish onto the shore. "This one's for him. We'll split the other two with everyone else."

She grabbed the fish, unhooked it, and threw it toward the approaching bear. The bear's large, dark form moved steadily closer down the rocky beach, drawn in by the two fishermen but easily distracted by the scent of the fresh catch. Its keen senses locked onto the offering, and it hesitated, considering the unexpected gift.

Meanwhile, Olivia and Henry acted fast, collecting their gear and their catch. Together, they quickly made their way toward the trail to camp. Olivia's heart pounded with adrenaline as the sound of leaves crunched under her steps. She hoped the bear would be happy with her gift and choose to leave them alone.

It wasn't.

She glanced back, her eyes meeting the bear's gaze before it fixated on the flopping fish, devouring it in a single act. The bear's intense focus shifted from the fish to Olivia, making direct eye contact again.

Olivia stared back, trying to suppress her nervousness and project an aura of calmness in hopes the bear would recognize it and retreat. The tension between them hung in the air, their eyes locked for what felt like an eternity. Then, the bear began edging closer, one step after another.

Unaware of the impending danger, Henry continued onward from the lake toward camp. Olivia's voice pierced the air as she called out, "Henry, he's coming this way!"

He halted in his tracks and slowly turned around. Olivia hastily retreated toward him, her gaze never leaving the bear as it gradually closed the distance between them.

"Ahh! Why is it following us, and how do we make it stop?" Henry said, his voice panicked.

"I don't know!" Standing beside him, she half-jokingly asked, "How fast can you run?"

He briefly diverted his attention from the approaching danger to glance at Olivia's smirking face.

"Very funny," he retorted. "But seriously, it's coming straight at us."

Olivia's heart pounded in her chest as the bear continued its steady approach. The creature's massive body seemed to fill the surrounding space. Its thick, dark fur glistened under the sunlight filtering through the trees. Its powerful legs carried it with an almost majestic grace, each step creating a soft thud that resonated in the otherwise quiet wilderness.

As the looming presence of the predator drew near, she instinctively reached for her empty belt where her bear spray should have rested—a nerve-racking realization settling in. Olivia had encountered many bears in the wild before, but this time was different.

When she spotted a pile of rocks nearby, her eyes lit up with an idea. "Grab some rocks! We have to try to scare it away," she exclaimed.

He noticed the rocks and swiftly grabbed a handful. Together, they stood their ground, raising their arms to appear larger and more threatening, while also preparing themselves to release a barrage of stones.

As the bear drew closer, tension reached its peak. "Now!" Olivia yelled and, in a synchronized motion, they hurled the rocks at the bear, hoping it would be enough to stop the predator and save their lives. Each rock sailed through the air, landing with a thud as it struck the bear, one after another.

Startled by the sudden assault, the bear froze. Seizing the moment, Olivia and Henry continued their aggressive shouts and threw rock after rock, enforcing their dominance over the territory.

The bear stood up on two legs, towering over them as it locked in on its foes. To its dismay, this didn't change the duo's approach and the bear dropped back down to all fours. Its massive frame then turned away, and with surprising agility, it sprinted off into the wilderness. Olivia and Henry remained breathless.

Relief washed over Olivia, knowing their actions successfully deterred the curious creature. The forest seemed to exhale alongside them as the tension dissipated, leaving the birds to return to their singing.

With the immediate danger averted, Olivia and Henry caught their breath and surveyed the area. She glanced at the rocks they had thrown and laughed. "We did it, Henry! We scared the bear off."

His eyes met hers, and his face read of relief and exhaustion. "I can't believe everything around here is trying to kill us," he said with a smirk.

Olivia chuckled, her hands shaking with adrenaline. "Well, it's all part of the adventure, right? And hey, we can add 'scaring off a bear' to our survival resumes now."

# 21

Upon returning to the rock formation, Olivia gestured to an area away from their camp, the lake, and the bear. "Let's set up a cooking station over there. I don't want to give that bear any reason to visit us in the middle of the night."

"I couldn't agree more," Henry said, setting down the fishing equipment and eagerly following her to the edge of the rocky clearing.

Olivia arranged a small fire ring using rocks lying in the vicinity, just like she did the night prior. She positioned two large rocks on either side of the fire pit and attempted to lay a large flat rock across the entire pit to create a makeshift stove, but it was too heavy to lift on her own.

"Here, let me help," Henry said as he reached down and grabbed one side of the rock. Olivia grabbed the other, and the two heaved the rock up into place.

She made her way back to the main camp, where a few glowing coals remained in the pit. Adding fresh sticks and logs, she rekindled the flames and ignited a new blaze. She placed a long stick into the fire and patiently waited for it to hold a flame.

"Hey, Henry!" she yelled out. "Could you gather a handful of kindling for that fire pit?"

"Absolutely."

She watched from a distance as Henry gathered smaller sticks and grass, arranging them under the rock in the second fire pit. With the now inflamed stick in hand, she walked it over to the cooking pit, carefully placing it atop the kindling. The flame eagerly spread, growing stronger with each second. Gradually, she added a couple of larger pieces beneath the rock.

Once the larger wood settled into a steady burn, she gently waved her hand over the rock, gauging its temperature. When the heat became unbearable, she knew it was the perfect temperature.

"Let's get those fish cooking. The fire is just right, and the others should be back soon," Olivia said.

Henry sat the first fish down, which sizzled on the hot rock, its tantalizing aroma wafting through the air.

Olivia's mouth watered with anticipation as she watched the fish's skin crisp and crackle to perfection.

Suddenly, the serene atmosphere was interrupted by the gentle rustling of foliage, drawing their attention. Amidst the trees, two familiar figures emerged, returning from their expedition.

"Over here! We've got dinner cooking," Henry called out.

"Mmm, that smells delicious, and boy, do I have a story for you two," Owen exclaimed. Alongside him, Lee approached with noticeable restraints, his hands bound with torn bits of clothing and his mouth gagged.

Olivia's optimism faded at the sight of Lee's makeshift bindings, her emotions swirling with concern, curiosity, and a touch of apprehension as she wondered what had transpired on their expedition. Her mind raced with questions, pondering the events that unfolded during their journey.

"What's happening?" she asked.

Owen's gaze met hers before he took a deep breath. "I'll explain everything," he said, his voice steady.

# 22

Owen positioned Lee against a nearby tree and found a place to sit alongside the others. "You two caught fish? That's impressive."

"We did," Henry chimed in, a note of pride in his voice. "Olivia whittled a fly rod."

Olivia turned her attention toward Owen, her focus unaffected by the compliment. "What happened? Why is Lee tied up?"

The flickering flames of the fire cast an eerie glow on Lee, deepening the shadows around his eyes. Owen's posture stiffened and he took a deep breath.

"We were climbing toward the summit when we reached a fork in the trail," he began. His voice remained steady, but his eyes were intense behind the shadows. "Lee wanted to split up to cover more ground. I was okay with that. At first, I planned to take the left path, but he insisted on going that way. He was really weird about it, but I couldn't quite pinpoint why. It was like he had a reason to go down that path or at least to keep me from it, and I couldn't shake that feeling."

The crackling of the fire punctuated Owen's words. Olivia and Henry exchanged glances. Olivia leaned in, her eyes now locked on Owen, silently urging him to continue.

He shifted his body and continued, "I stood my ground and insisted on taking the left trail. After a brief back and forth, he agreed to go right. I made my way down the left path, and maybe a few hundred yards later, I heard cries for help. I could recognize that voice anywhere. It was Terry."

Olivia's voice barely above a whisper, "What happened next?"

"I ran toward him through the trees," Owen recounted, his voice trembling. "When I found him, my heart dropped. Somehow, Terry had managed to work a bloodstained gag off his mouth, and he was desperately calling for help. I reassured him, untied the rest of the cloth, and that's when he looked me right in the eye and said, 'Lee did this to me.'"

The weight of those words lingered, filling the space with an overwhelming sense of betrayal. Olivia's eyes widened, her mind grappling with the shocking revelation.

Her gaze shifted toward Lee. To her astonishment, he violently shook his head in disagreement as his muffled protests were drowned out by the gag.

Undeterred, Owen pressed on, "Suddenly, I felt a sharp thud against the back of my head, and I rolled down the hill. My vision was blurry, but I watched as Lee walked over to Terry. I was still pretty out of it, but I realized he must have been the one who hit me. I tried to yell at him, but as I did, he picked up a log and swung it at Terry."

Olivia and Henry both gasped.

Owen let out a heavy sigh. Her heart raced and her chest grew tight. This had become a nightmare beyond anything she could have ever imagined.

"I stood up, shook off the dizziness, and lunged at him. But he ran off, like a coward. I looked over at Terry's lifeless body, and the rage took over. So, I chased after him. He was fast, dodging through game trails, climbing over ridgelines, and jumping logs, but after around thirty minutes, I caught him. I tackled him and, well, to be honest, I punched him in the face a few times. My rage just took over. Eventually, I calmed down and tied him up."

Olivia's emotions churned as she absorbed Owen's words. *Terry is dead? Lee is a killer? Is this real?* The image of Lee being subdued and the expression of fury on Owen's face was etched into her mind.

"At that point, I had no clue where we were," he continued. "The undergrowth is so thick. All I knew was that finding Terry was the priority. So, I dragged Lee around for hours, trying to find any sign of him, but I couldn't find that spot. Eventually, I knew I needed to head back down the mountain to camp. But, yeah, Lee kidnapped and killed Terry."

Olivia felt her chest constrict and beads of sweat formed around her hairline as a tidal wave of anxiety crashed over her upon hearing those words. She sat there, stunned and overwhelmed, struggling to articulate the storm of emotions raging within her. Despite her best efforts, the right words eluded her, slipping through her grasp like sand. She was paralyzed, unable to process or understand what had just happened.

After a few moments of silence, Henry asked, "Well, what now? We're stranded here, without a satellite phone or any means of communication, and now we have a murderer among us. Any ideas on what we should do next?"

Owen brazenly retrieved a handful of cooked trout from the fire, devouring it within seconds. With a satisfied expression, he shifted his gaze toward Olivia and Henry.

"We need to make sure Lee is restrained and can't hurt anyone else. Once I feel confident in that, I can focus on finding a way out of here."

"That's a good first step," Henry said.

Owen proceeded to the main campfire and retrieved a knife and the paracord. With a determined look, he made his way to Lee, forcefully dragged him back to the main camp area, and threw him onto the ground.

The venom in Owen's voice was unmistakable as he addressed his captive, "Are you comfortable? I hope not, because you're going to be here for a while, scumbag."

Owen worked methodically, each move deliberate and precise. He started with a large boulder and carefully wrapped the cord around it, securing it under Lee's armpits and directly across his chest. He completed ten tight wraps before testing it. It didn't budge. He tied it off at the back and cut the excess.

He turned his attention to Lee's hands, untying the makeshift restraints from Lee's shirt sleeves. In their place, he bound them with paracord, firmly locking his hands into place.

Continuing his systematic approach, he seized both of Lee's ankles. Replicating the actions performed on his hands, he wrapped the cord around each ankle, then together, securing them tightly. To ensure further restraint, Owen tied one of Lee's ankles to another nearby rock, leaving no possibility of escape.

With Lee now securely bound and unable to cause an issue, Owen stepped away from the scene and joined the others near the crackling fire.

Olivia needed time to gather her thoughts. Excusing herself quietly, she rose from her seat and began a slow, solitary stroll away from camp. Without a word, Henry got up and joined her.

# 23

Olivia and Henry quietly traversed the thick timber until they were far enough away to speak freely. The pair continued another hundred yards until finally arriving at a small opening in the trees, a temporary refuge from the magnitude of their reality.

Exhausted, both physically and emotionally, Olivia collapsed into Henry's arms. Tears streamed down her face as the overwhelming weight of Owen's story and the harrowing truth of their predicament became too much to bear. The unrestrained sobs echoed through the stillness of the forest.

Once the tension subsided and Olivia regained control, she gently pulled away from Henry's embrace. She felt the puffiness around her eyes and the coolness on her saturated cheeks. *I must look as terrible as I feel right now.*

In a quivering voice, she posed the question that had been haunting her, "What are we going to do? Terry is gone, and with him, the satellite phone. And now, to make matters worse, we have a murderer among us."

Henry's eyes, usually bright and filled with life, carried an unmistakable fatigue. The lines etched on his forehead cried of the burden he carried. The weight of their situation had taken its toll. Henry appeared defeated and distant in the moment.

She struggled to find the right words to encourage him, but then a glimmer of hope sparked within her.

"Henry, we will make it home. It's going to happen. You will meet your grandchild, I promise."

As she uttered those words, the twinkle returned to his eyes. It was as if a switch had been flipped, and his demeanor shifted from defeat to determination.

"But how?"

"I don't know yet, but we'll find a way. Let's talk about that story Owen told us first though. It's so bizarre. Why would Lee do something like that?"

"I don't know. I don't know much about Lee, but I can't imagine he would want Terry dead. He seems as eager as we are to get out of here. It's all so strange. At this moment, I trust you, and you alone."

"Agreed. We need to be cautious here," Olivia said. "That means we shouldn't take everything Owen says as truth. Let's see if we can get more information. Are you okay if we head back and see what else we can find out?"

"Of course. Let's get to the bottom of this."

# 24

Upon returning to camp, Olivia nestled into her spot near the fire. She immediately turned her attention toward Owen and asked, "What do we do now? We don't have a satellite phone, and no one knows where we are."

Henry joined in, echoing Olivia's sentiment, "I'd like to know as well. My wife must be worried sick about me, and as much as I'm enjoying getting to know you, I want to get out of here."

Owen met their concerned gaze. "We have to hike out. It's our only option. It will be tough, over fifty miles, I imagine. We can do it, but we need to be prepared."

His plan began to take shape as he continued, "Tomorrow, the two of you focus on catching as many fish as possible and smoke them too. That way we can safely take them with us. I'll make another pass of the area and search for Terry's body and that satellite phone. If I can't find that phone, we'll need to leave here the next morning."

Olivia nodded before she rose from her seat, seized a handful of fish and her water bottle, and headed toward Lee.

"Don't feed that creep!" Owen shouted.

She glanced back, shaking her head in disagreement. "I won't let him die out here," she asserted. "He's a person, and I'll treat him as one, regardless of what he's done."

Owen didn't respond, allowing her to proceed toward Lee undeterred. She knelt beside him and untied the sleeve that gagged his mouth. As she fed him, he whispered, "He made the whole thing up. He's lying, I swear. I can prove it too."

Olivia was torn between Lee's pleas and the weight of Owen's account. Was there a chance Lee was telling the truth and Owen had misled them all? The uncertainty gnawed at her, but she maintained her flat demeanor.

She continued to feed Lee in silence. He followed a bite with a plea, "Please believe me. I didn't do anything."

As doubts and questions continued to swirl within her mind, she grappled with the gravity of the situation. If Lee's claims were true, it meant Owen could be an immensely dangerous individual. This realization compelled her to be extra cautious and guarded with her thoughts and suspicions, and she prayed Henry would do the same.

After feeding Lee the last of the fish, she assisted him as he took a drink of water. As she prepared to secure his gag, he begged once more, "I swear, Olivia, don't trust him. It was all him."

She hesitated, torn between his words and the complexity of the situation. However, she knew she had to remain neutral, so she tightly secured the gag.

Afterward, she focused on his comfort and survival. She gathered a generous stack of spruce branches from the bedding area and arranged them around him for insulation from the chill of the night. She then built a small fire nearby before carefully placing a large log on it to smolder throughout the night.

Satisfied with her efforts, she stepped back. Her attention shifted to Henry and Owen, who had made their way back to the main camp. "There, now at least he'll survive the night," she said.

"Thank you for being civil," Henry said sincerely.

Olivia smiled at Henry before taking a bite of fish and turning toward Owen, fully committed to the plan at hand. She was careful not to let Owen sense any doubt or suspicion in her words.

"That sounds like a solid plan to me, Owen. Henry and I will focus on fishing and smoking trout tomorrow. Meanwhile, please find Terry and the satellite phone."

A sparkle of relief engulfed his face. "Agreed. Let's call it a night and rest up. We have a tough journey ahead of us."

As the camp settled into the tranquil embrace of night, Olivia's thoughts raged like a tempest. Questions and uncertainties clamored for attention, demanding resolution. Unfortunately, that would have to wait.

In the flickering glow of the fire, she replayed the events of the day, her mind a detective piecing together fragments of information. Lee's words gave her pause. She continued to question his motives, wondering if his plea was genuine or a desperate lie. Yet, she couldn't ignore what she had witnessed between Owen and Terry, their frequent disagreements and clashes. Henry noticed the same as well. They had to be on to something.

As she contemplated her next move, she vowed to proceed with the utmost caution. She would observe and listen, seeking the subtle signs that might reveal the truth. Each interaction—each word spoken—would be scrutinized for any hint of deception or manipulation.

In the stillness of the night, Olivia's resolve grew stronger. She closed her eyes, finding solace in the fire's warmth. The challenges ahead would test her, but she would be prepared.

# 25

Sunlight crested over the mountain and plunged into camp. Olivia was already awake; nightmares had ended her slumber hours ago. She had accepted it and silently obsessed over every detail of the last few days.

Since morning had officially arrived, the others began to wake. Olivia decided to check on Lee. As she peeked over at him, he raised his head toward her. His eyes reflected the same sentiment as before, but there was nothing she could do for him. Not yet anyway. Not without more information.

Owen fumbled to his spot by the fire pit and was joined by Henry. Olivia followed and was greeted with a smile.

"Morning," Henry said.

"Good morning. Let's hope it's our last one here."

"I sure hope so," Owen added.

"How many fish do you think we need to catch today?" Henry asked.

"Well, we'll be lucky to get five, maybe ten, miles tops a day in this terrain, so I'm guessing we'll make it to town in six days max. Half a fish a day each." A mischievous smile crept across Olivia's face as she watched him tally the numbers on his fingers. "I think nine or ten fish should do it," Owen concluded.

"There are four of us. Lee is coming with us," Olivia firmly stated.

Owen sighed in frustration and muttered, "Fine, let's call it twelve. But if that scum falls behind, we're leaving him."

Olivia brushed off his response and collected the fishing gear. Henry joined her.

"Twelve trout coming right up," he said with a smile.

"If you only get nine, I know who won't get any," Owen said as his smile turned into laughter.

Olivia instinctively shot him an annoyed look. But she reminded herself to conceal her discontent, knowing that revealing her doubts could jeopardize their fragile unity and set Owen down a war path.

Oblivious to her suspicions, Owen asked, "Can I have a granola bar? I'll be out all day searching for Terry and could use the fuel."

Olivia seized the opportunity to save face and happily handed it to him. She attempted some additional goodwill by adding in a somber tone, "I'm sorry about Terry. I hope you find him."

Owen let her condolences sink in. His face softened before saying, "I appreciate that. We've had our fair share of bickering, but deep down, we were great friends. I'm going to give it my all to find him and make things right."

As Olivia and Henry walked toward the lake, carrying their fishing gear, Olivia turned to him and in a low voice asked, "This all still feels so off. When I went over to Lee last night, he whispered to me that he didn't do it."

Henry's eyes widened. "He told you that? Interesting. Let's take him at his word for a moment. That means if Lee is innocent, then Owen made the whole thing up and blamed it on him. Why would he do that?"

"Right. I'm still trying to make sense of it all and find a motive for Lee, but nothing adds up. On the other hand, Owen. There are plenty of reasons why he might want Terry to go missing."

Henry paused. "Exactly. We saw how Terry treated him, always blaming him for every little thing that went wrong. It's not far-fetched to think Owen saw an opportunity to remove Terry from the equation and took it. It makes way more sense than it does if it were Lee."

The pieces of the puzzle were coming together for Olivia, and her doubts about Owen's version of events solidified. At this point, she was almost certain they were being manipulated, that the truth was being distorted. It was time to uncover the reality behind their predicament.

She reached for Henry's shoulder and stopped, locking eyes with him. "Henry," she said softly, "I trust you. Do you trust me?"

"Yes. I trust you completely."

"Great. Can you handle catching all the fish on your own?"

"I might be here a while, but I think I can handle it."

"Great, do you know how to build a smoker?"

"Yeah, I do. I've seen enough survival shows to understand the concept. I'll just add some walls to that cooking setup with some additional rocks and cover it with some spruce needles. That should work."

Olivia's attention shifted toward the camp, her mind decided. "Sounds good to me. I'm going to follow Owen and find out what's going on."

"Be careful. If we're right, he's dangerous," Henry said.

"I will. Trust me, we'll get to the bottom of this."

# 26

Olivia snuck her way back to camp, each step intentional to avoid making a sound. As she approached camp, she hid behind a large shrub and watched Owen lace his boots up to prepare for his search. He grabbed a water bottle and went down the same path he had taken the day prior.

As she followed him, she moved with the skill of a seasoned tracker, her years of hunting experience with her father now proving invaluable. When he slowed down or stopped, she tucked herself behind a tree or shrub to avoid detection. What little sound she did make was drowned out by the forest, which seemed to come alive around her. Birds sang, trees rustled together in the wind, and Owen's whistling concealed her movements.

Owen paused and Olivia cautiously took a knee behind a tree. He was taking longer than expected to decide which path he needed to take. While she waited for him to continue, she glanced down and noticed she narrowly avoided a mound of bear scat. The sight sent chills down her spine as she recalled her intense encounter with the bear the day before. Her memory of its fierce growls and piercing gaze was still fresh.

Then it dawned on her. While she and Henry had successfully scared it off yesterday, who knew how another encounter would fare? Without her being there, how would Henry fare alone? She hoped she wouldn't find out, but she couldn't worry about that now. She needed to concentrate on the task at hand as Owen headed down another path.

Continuing her pursuit, she noted Owen's footsteps were noisy, and he constantly whistled as he walked, making it relatively easy for her to track him deeper into the woods. As he veered off the main trail onto smaller game paths and then onto even narrower ones, her concern grew. The unfamiliar territory raised the possibility of getting lost.

To mitigate the risk, she picked up a unique-looking stick and placed it at each trail intersection, creating a series of markers indicating the direction she came from. This was the same method she had used with Henry during their earlier hike and many times before that.

Suddenly, Owen halted, prompting Olivia to drop to a knee once more. Her heart pounded so loud it distracted her until Owen's voice thundered through the forest, startling her attention back to Owen. "Alright, old man, where did you hide that satellite phone?"

Relief washed over Olivia when she heard Terry's voice. "I should have never trusted you," he said. His voice sounded tired, but it was filled with anger. "I knew you were a snake from the start. I should have dropped you from my operation a long time ago."

Owen's laughter echoed ominously through the trees as she watched him lean in closer. "But you didn't. And worst of all, you tried to outsmart me. I found your stash, the one hidden behind the boxes in your closet. I don't like to be lied to, Terry. Fifty-fifty partner? Ha! Not then, and from now on, everything's mine. No one will ever hear from you again."

Olivia took three calculated steps and spotted Terry. His shirt collar was stained red and covered in dirt. He didn't have his hat, and his hair was matted with dried blood. His pants were destroyed with large rips down the left leg and both of his sleeves were missing. Paracord stretched across his chest, binding him to a tree.

The sight urged Olivia to intervene, confront Owen, and save Terry from further harm. However, a nagging voice of caution reminded her of Owen's physical strength and the potential danger she would be putting herself into.

Should she act now, risking her safety in an attempt to rescue Terry? Or should she wait, go get both Henry and Lee and then confront him? The debate raged within her, torn between the urgency to protect Terry and the need to ensure her survival.

"What's the matter, old man? Nothing to say for yourself?" Owen said. "How about you redeem yourself a bit and tell me where you hid that satellite phone? What do you say?"

Terry's eyes burned with defiance as he held Owen's gaze. His voice, barely audible, carried a determination as he murmured, "Have fun trying to find your way out of here. I don't have the phone on me, and I'll never tell you where I stashed it."

Olivia was instantly relieved to hear this. It meant there was still hope, that Terry still held a lifeline to the world. A way to escape.

Owen's chest slowly rose and fell as he took several breaths and leaned against a nearby tree. He glared down at Terry like a lion watching over his fallen prey. For a few moments, they locked eyes, their silent confrontation speaking volumes. Terry may have fallen, but he was far from broken.

Owen's gaze broke first. "I have all day. No one's expecting me back to camp until dark, so if you want to play this game, I'll play it." He reached down and picked up a pebble. With a fast twitch of his arm, he launched it at Terry's chest. "Next one gets bigger. The one after that, even bigger."

Owen then pointed to a nearby boulder, its size resembling that of an ATV tire. "It all ends with that one. Tell me where the phone is."

Terry remained silent, his resolve unyielding, and kept his eyes locked on his adversary.

After witnessing the tense interaction, Olivia knew she had to regroup with the others back at camp. Rising to her feet, she made sure to remain as quiet as possible. Carefully, she took a small step backward.

With utmost caution, she retraced her path, relying on her trail markings to guide her. Time was of the essence though, and she knew she had to act swiftly while avoiding any hint that she had ever been present.

After putting a safe distance between herself and Owen, she allowed herself to pause and take a deep breath. This new information hit her like a wave crashing against the shore, bringing her down to her knees. *Terry is alive.* She sighed with relief. She couldn't recall the last time she had taken a breath since discovering him.

But amid this, a surge of anger swelled within her. Owen had turned Terry into a prisoner and manipulated everyone, blaming it all on Lee. The pieces were starting to come together in her mind: the plane crash, this whole fiasco. It all seemed like a calculated ploy orchestrated by Owen to confront Terry about his mistreatment in some operation they were involved in.

Rage ignited within her as she swore to bring him to justice. But before she could do that, she needed to reunite with Henry and Lee. With her newfound determination propelling her, she sprinted toward camp, her heart set on ensuring Owen paid for his actions behind bars.

# 27

Olivia's footsteps felt heavy as she trudged back into camp, her mind still in shock from what she had just witnessed. As she approached, she noticed Henry standing beside a pile of freshly caught and smoked fish.

"Pretty successful morning, I'd say. I'm just breaking down the smoker now. I didn't reel in anything much bigger than my hand, but the fishing was incredible. On the bright side, smoking them didn't take long at all, only about an hour or so." His smile faded when he saw the turmoil etched on her face. "You don't look too good, what happened?"

"We need to untie Lee."

Henry's eyes widened as he processed her words. "Why? What happened?"

She inhaled sharply and gathered herself before responding, "Terry," she said. "I found him. He's still alive, and Owen is torturing him right now, demanding the location of the satellite phone."

She walked over to Lee, who was still bound but attentive to every word she said. He nodded, confirming the truth in her words and what he had been trying to convey all along.

"Wait," Henry interjected. "Tell me more first. Up until a minute ago, I thought this man was a murderer. Walk me through everything."

Olivia recognized the complexity of the situation, of Henry's understandable confusion, but time was ticking. She grabbed him by the shoulders and asked, "Do you trust me?"

Meeting her gaze, he nervously scratched his head. "Yes, Olivia. I trust you."

"Good," she said firmly. "We don't have much time. I'll explain everything on the way. We have an hour's hike ahead of us if we ever want to see Terry alive again."

Seemingly satisfied with that response, Henry followed her as she offered Lee a genuine apology and removed the gag tied around his mouth.

Lee rubbed his face with his hands. "Thank you. I wasn't sure if you believed me yesterday."

"Honestly, I didn't. You got me thinking, but I've also had my reservations about you since we boarded the plane."

Henry relaxed his shoulders. "Yeah, your first impression didn't exactly win us over."

Lee let out a sigh. "I get it. I know my first impressions are never the best. This trip has been especially rough for me professionally, and honestly, I just wanted to go home. That's why I kept to myself and didn't engage with either of you."

"It's okay, but something about Owen didn't sit right with me either," she admitted. "He was so nonchalant about Terry going missing."

Henry chimed in, "And there was a lot of bickering and name-calling between the two, which felt off."

"That too. When I thought about the whole scenario and the story Owen spun up, it just didn't make sense," Olivia said. "Lee, I couldn't think of one valid motive for you to commit murder in this situation. It just simply didn't add up."

"Thank you for seeing through the lies," Lee said. "You mentioned Terry's in trouble and something about a long hike. Let's get going. I'll share everything that happened with Owen on the way."

"Yeah, let's go," Olivia agreed. She walked over to where she had left her hatchet and picked it up before securing it around her belt.

Henry watched her and, with a hint of concern in his voice, commented, "I really hope you don't intend on using that for anything."

"I don't, but I'd rather have it just in case."

## 28

As they hurried down the trail, Olivia led, but her attention was focused on Lee's words as he shared his side of the story. She wanted to understand every detail, to piece together the puzzle that had brought them to this point.

"I was following Owen on a trail, hoping we might find Terry at the summit or at least some signs of him," Lee said. "I had the same hopes as you two until we reached a fork in the trail. That's when Owen's behavior took a strange turn. He seemed agitated and started rambling. I tried to reason with him, explaining the best approach was one way, but he insisted on going the opposite way."

Olivia exchanged a concerned glance with Henry as Lee continued, "I decided to trust my instincts and told him we should split up and he should go his way. As I continued on the trail in the direction I believed was right, I felt a sharp thud on the back of my head. I must have been hit by a large stick or rock. The next thing I knew, I woke up and Owen was standing above me, tying my hands together."

Henry scrunched his forehead as he processed the information. "So, Owen attacked you and used you as a scapegoat for Terry's disappearance?" he questioned.

Lee nodded. "I think so. I imagine I was pretty close to finding Terry and he didn't want that. So, he set me up, making it seem like I was responsible for Terry's disappearance. But I swear, I had nothing to do with it. I'm just as desperate as you to find a way out of here."

Olivia's grip tightened around the hatchet. Her knuckles turned white as anger surged through her. "That's the exact story he fed us, just the characters twisted."

"He really lacks imagination, doesn't he?" Henry said.

"He does. Then he went on to tell me everything. About how he lured Terry away from camp that night. How he intended on pinning it all on me and ensuring you two remained oblivious. I guess he wants to get rid of Terry, take all his money, and then vanish without a trace," Lee said.

Henry's eyes widened. "Wait, what money? Terry is a pilot; there can't be much money there. What are you talking about?"

Olivia turned to him. "I overheard something earlier. Owen mentioned Terry was hiding money from him—something about an operation they were involved in. I didn't catch all the details, but it seems Owen found out, and that's what started all of this."

Lee lowered his head. "I don't know anything about the money or the operation. Owen never mentioned any of that to me. All I know is he was determined to pin everything on me."

Olivia's jaw clenched and her anger intensified. "We need to figure out the whole truth and let the police deal with them."

Henry's expression hardened. "I can't believe he would go to such lengths. We can't let him get away with this."

"I know," Lee said. "That's why I'm glad you two are here. Together, we'll take him down."

Henry turned to Lee. "We're sorry we didn't believe you earlier. We should have trusted you from the start."

"It's okay," Lee reassured. "I understand why you were skeptical, but I'm just glad you can see the truth now."

"Yeah, me too. Now let's go save Terry and put a stop to Owen's plan," Olivia said.

# 29

As the group trudged on, the tension in the air grew. The hike felt longer to Olivia than before as her mind raced with thoughts of potential scenarios, meticulously analyzing each one. The weight of the impending confrontation with Owen weighed heavily on her, and she couldn't shake off the nerves.

"We have to stay cautious," she advised the others. "We should find Terry alive and confront Owen, but I have no idea how he'll react. He could run away, or he could try to fight us."

"You're right," Henry said. "We have to be prepared for whatever comes our way. But let's hope he chooses to run away, and we can end this without resorting to violence."

As the group spotted the first marker Olivia created, they knew they were on the right track.

"We're close," she announced. She gripped the wooden handle of her hatchet in anticipation.

Lee stopped abruptly, his eyes sweeping over the area to ensure no one else could hear them. "We're ready to do what needs to be done here, right? Owen will not get away with this."

Olivia drew in a deep breath, her gaze steady. "In my head, I am. I've never been in a fight before, so if that comes to that, I hope I have the courage to do what I need to do to keep everyone safe. I'm pretty sure I do."

Henry placed a reassuring hand on her shoulder. "You're not alone in this," he said. "We're here too, and we all want the same thing. I have no doubt that the three of us will prevail. We'll face whatever happens together."

As the group ventured further down the trail, Olivia searched for the next trail marker. Finally, she spotted it, barely visible among the dense foliage and towering trees but obvious to her. She halted and turned to face the others. "This is the last marker," she whispered. "They're only a few hundred feet away."

The gravity of the moment hung heavy in the air. Olivia's chest tightened and her palms were sweaty as she observed each of her companions' appearances and body language. Henry appeared equally nervous, his hands fidgeting as he rubbed the back of his neck. Lee, on the other hand, appeared surprisingly calm and collected, his posture relaxed as he maintained a vigilant watch on their surroundings.

His demeanor became a source of reassurance for Olivia, prompting her to pause and regain her composure. She briefly closed her eyes, taking multiple deep breaths to steady her frayed nerves.

"Take a moment, Olivia. We'll go when you're ready," Lee said as he patted her shoulder.

Olivia continued to compose herself. She focused on her breathing, drawing strength from the surrounding nature. The rustling leaves and distant chirping of birds served as a serene backdrop to the sound she was looking for—the faint murmur of voices that emanated from deeper in the woods.

She took a few steps closer until the sound of Owen's voice became clearer. "Alright, Terry, I see where this is going. I'd really like that phone, but it doesn't look like you're going to give it up."

Olivia exchanged a glance with the others. They heard Owen's words as well. It was time to make their move.

"We need to get closer," she whispered, her voice barely audible. "Stay low and follow my lead. We have to act fast to catch him off guard."

The others nodded in understanding, ready to enact the plan. They moved stealthily through the undergrowth, each step calculated and precise to avoid stepping on a single twig or leaf.

Owen continued, his voice growing impatient, "Terry, we're not going to do this all day. This is a pretty big rock. Are you sure you want me to drop that on your head?"

The three exchanged glances once more.

Olivia waved to Henry and Lee to stay behind her, her grip on the hatchet's handle firm. She stepped forward out of the trees and revealed herself to Owen.

"Owen, we know everything. The gig's up."

He looked up, clearly caught off guard by her sudden appearance. Panic flashed across his face as he stammered, "I found Terry! He's alive. He says he has the satellite phone too. We're safe!"

Terry's eyes widened with a mixture of disbelief as he watched Olivia approach. His face was covered in dried blood and bruises. Despite being beaten, battered, and broken, a glimmer of hope shone in his eyes.

Henry and Lee walked up behind Olivia and the trio confronted Owen. Their determined gazes locked onto the man who had orchestrated such chaos and pain. Owen's face twisted in rage. His eyes, once filled with a sense of superiority, now revealed a hint of fear as he realized he had been caught.

"Stay back. I'm not afraid of the three of you," he spat out.

Olivia's heart thundered in her chest as her emotions ran high. Her nerves were on edge as she tightened her grip once more on her hatchet. Seeking reassurance, she glanced at Henry and Lee, finding strength in their support.

Terry tried to sit up but collapsed, his body betrayed by the ordeal he had endured. Olivia's heart ached for him. She wanted to help him, but she knew she had to stay focused on the immediate threat.

Olivia unsheathed her hatchet and prepared herself. With her jaw clenched and a burning fire in her eyes, she took a step forward.

Lee and Henry mirrored her, standing side by side, united and ready for whatever came their way.

As Owen frantically lunged forward, screaming, Olivia stood her ground. In a desperate attempt to throw them off, Owen hurled handfuls of dirt and gravel at the group. Lee and Henry shielded their faces, but Olivia managed to keep her eyes locked on him, refusing to let his scare tactics get the best of her.

As he charged forward, Olivia's adrenaline surged and she swung the hatchet, narrowly missing him. He dodged but lunged again and tackled her to the ground, aiming to disarm her. She fought back and Henry and Lee quickly stepped in to help.

Owen jumped up and swung at Henry, connecting with his jaw. Henry, stunned, fell back. Lee restrained Owen, but he slipped out of his range. The struggle continued. In the chaos, adrenaline coursed through Olivia, her breaths coming in labored gasps.

She aimed her hatchet at Owen once again, but before she could swing, Henry recovered and tackled him to the ground. The two rolled down the hillside, grappling fiercely.

Owen managed to break away and fled, scrambling as he disappeared into the wilderness. Olivia, Henry, and Lee were left standing, panting, and shaken—but victorious. They had prevailed against Owen's aggression.

Olivia turned her attention toward Terry, who was lying on the ground. She approached him and asked, "Are you okay?"

With a weak smile, Terry replied, "I'll live."

As he spoke, Olivia noticed the cuts and swelling on his face. She sliced the paracord that bound him to the tree and handed him her water bottle. He gratefully accepted it and drank the entire contents. "Let's go to camp."

"Please tell me you have the satellite phone. I'm not looking forward to walking out of here," she said.

"Yeah, I hid it back at camp."

"Oh, thank goodness!" Henry exclaimed.

Lee asked, "Why did you hide it?"

"I had my suspicions about Owen and wanted to make sure it was safe. How do you misread a date on a paper? That just didn't sit right with me, and I've known him for a long time. I could tell something was eating at him and, with him being pretty impulsive, I thought he might try something."

"Are you good to get up?" Olivia asked.

Terry made an effort to rise on his own, but his legs gave out. Olivia and Henry rushed to offer their support.

"Take it easy, Terry," Henry said. "We'll help you back."

Terry was visibly exhausted, but he was determined. He tried to stand once more with their help. His legs trembled, and he stumbled a few more times before finding his balance. "Thanks," he murmured. "I think I'm okay to hike back."

Olivia and Henry exchanged concerned glances, neither remotely convinced.

"Should we go after Owen?" Henry asked.

"No, a bear will get to him. There's no way he makes it out of here alive, and if he does, I'll be waiting for him," Terry said.

# 30

When they arrived back at camp, Terry collapsed by the fire pit. "I'm okay, just give me a minute," he said. Lee helped make him comfortable on the spruce needle bedding. Olivia sat next to them and sparked the fire back to life.

Meanwhile, Henry returned with the fish he had smoked earlier. "Looks like we're not going to hike out of here, so let's dig in and celebrate," he said, passing out the fish.

"Amen," Olivia chimed in as the realization of how hungry she was kicked in. She happily accepted a filet and savored every bite until it was gone.

Terry followed suit, finishing his fish before asking, "How?"

"All Olivia's doing," Henry said.

"That's not true. You caught and smoked each one of these fish."

"True, but without you, I wouldn't have had the means to do so."

"Thank you, both. And Lee, too. Not just for this, but for saving me. I think he was about to kill me," Terry said. He reached over and patted Olivia's leg. She embraced his hand before he pulled it away.

As hours passed, Terry's strength began to return, and he appeared refreshed with a newfound energy. "I'll be right back," he announced. He struggled to stand up.

Olivia asked, "Do you want someone to go with you? You've had quite the day."

"I'm fine. It'll just be a minute," Terry assured her, and he stumbled into the woods.

"Should someone follow him?" Henry asked, clearly concerned.

"Give it a few minutes. I'm sure he'll be okay," Lee said.

Silence consumed camp as they waited. They didn't wait long though because Terry returned within minutes, proudly displaying a satellite phone in his hand, his face beaming.

"Who's ready to call home and remember this dreadful experience from the comfort of their own living room?"

Olivia's face softened and she replied, "Thank goodness! I thought I'd never see a phone again. Wait, I'm guessing we still need to hike up to get service though, right?"

Terry frowned. "Yeah, we do. And this day's almost over, so it's looking like we unfortunately have one more night here."

"Only this time, we have to be worried about Owen's potential attack," Lee warned.

Olivia suggested a plan, proposing two-hour shifts. Lee and Henry both agreed to the idea.

Terry added after a moment of hesitation, "That's fine. We need to collect some firewood. After spending last night almost freezing to death, I really don't want to repeat that experience."

"Let's get to it then," Olivia said. "We should stay in pairs though. Owen could be anywhere, just waiting for one of us to stray away. Henry and I will head down this side trail, and the two of you can scavenge toward the lake. Let's plan to be back here in forty-five minutes."

Terry agreed with the plan and added, "If any of us aren't back by then, assume the worst and come find us."

Olivia led Henry along the trail system, heading toward a large fallen tree they had seen on their way back to camp with Terry.

As they walked, Henry suddenly stopped, prompting Olivia to turn and look at him. "This whole situation has been crazy. The plane crash, Terry missing, and now Owen is just out there somewhere. I'm struggling. How are you holding up?" he asked.

Olivia kept her eyes down on the trail, the weight of the situation weighing heavy on her mind. She could hear the unease in his voice, and she knew they were both grappling with the same overwhelming emotions.

"I won't lie," she began. "Despite Terry being back and it looking like we're on our way home, it's been a lot to handle. The crash, the uncertainty about Terry, and the unknown with Owen. It's all taking its toll."

Henry groaned. "I feel like I'm in a nightmare I can't wake up from."

"I know exactly how you feel. It's been an emotional rollercoaster, but I think it's okay to feel overwhelmed."

Henry let out a sigh. "I'm trying to stay strong, but it's hard. I just want this nightmare to end and for all of us to be safe."

Olivia clutched Henry's hand, giving it a firm squeeze. "We've got this. Tomorrow's call is our ticket out of here."

"I appreciate you being here," he said.

"Same here," she replied. "We've had each other's backs. Let's keep it that way and get out of here."

As they reached the large fallen tree, they began collecting firewood. The rhythm of the task brought a slight sense of normalcy amid the chaos, allowing them both to find some measure of peace. In that moment of tranquility, Olivia's drained emotional state made her mind wander, stirring up an unresolved issue.

With enough firewood collected for one load, they started back toward camp. "This whole situation is overwhelming," Olivia finally spoke, her voice vulnerable. "It reminds me of the darkest time in my life."

Henry turned to her. "What do you mean?"

She exhaled and gathered the courage to share. "I told you about James, right?"

"Yes."

"Did I tell you how he passed away?" she asked, her voice trembling as she stopped, dropped the wood she was carrying, and leaned against a tree for support.

"No, you haven't," he said, his eyes filled with empathy.

"It's the reason I moved up here." Her voice broke slightly. "We were heading back from an evening trip to the Lower Madison River. It's only a thirty-minute drive from town, so we went there often. The fishing has always been good to me there too." Memories of James flashed through her mind.

"Go on," Henry encouraged, gently squeezing her hand.

She collected herself once more before continuing, "Anyway, I was driving back, and this car..." She paused, tears welling up in her eyes. "This car came flying around a curve. A drunk driver. I tried my best to swerve away, but he hit us head-on."

Tears streamed down Olivia's face, and she struggled to continue. Henry pulled her into a hug.

"I woke up in a hospital," she said. "I had no idea what happened, so I started screaming. I looked down and an IV was sticking out of my arm. I ripped it off and tried to get out of bed, but I just crashed to the floor. Turns out I broke my leg, as well as a few other bones in my arm and foot.

"Three nurses stormed in and forced me back into bed. They shot me up with some kind of drug to calm me down. I'm not sure what it was, but it helped numb my mind and forced me to stop panicking. I wish I had some of that right now," she said, managing a small smile amid her tears.

"If I had any, it'd all be yours," he said softly.

"I'm sorry, Henry, I'm blabbering." She wiped away the tears from her face.

"Don't apologize. This is important and I have nowhere else to be but here with you. Literally, I'm stuck here."

Olivia half laughed and took another deep breath. "Once I finally calmed down enough to have a conversation, I asked the nurses about James. That's when they told me I was the only survivor." She choked back her sobs as tears cascaded down her cheeks.

Henry held her hand tightly.

"It felt like my world shattered," she continued, her voice still trembling. "I woke up alone in the hospital without him. I couldn't believe he was gone, and I felt so guilty for surviving when he didn't."

Tears flowed freely now, and Olivia found herself leaning into Henry's comforting presence.

"You don't have to carry that guilt. It's not your fault."

"I know," she whispered. "I tell myself that all the time, but it's hard not to feel that way sometimes. I miss him every day, and I wish there was something I could have done to save him."

"Sometimes life throws us into situations that are beyond our control. It's not fair, it's not our fault, and it's okay to grieve and feel the pain. But remember, you're not alone. I'm here for you, and so are your friends and family."

"Thank you for being here."

"You don't have to thank me," he replied, his eyes filled with warmth. "We've been through a lot together and I care about you. I'll always be here for you, no matter what."

Olivia withdrew from Henry and sat in the foliage deep in the woods. She wiped the tears from her cheeks. "Thank you. I feel much better. I've never actually told anyone that story. My family knows of course, but the words have never come out of my mouth. It's like a huge weight just left my soul."

Henry knelt beside her. "I know exactly how you feel, Olivia. I lost my sister a long time ago, and I carried that pain with me for many years. One day, similar to you, I started talking about her more, and I felt better. I found that the best way to remember someone is to talk about them. And let them motivate you to be your best version."

Those words resonated with Olivia, and she contemplated their meaning. "I like that. It's a great way to think of it. I've been running from everything for so long now, but I think that's only made it worse. James wouldn't want me to roll up in a ball and hide from the world. He'd want me to be the best version of myself, wouldn't he?"

Henry stood up and outstretched a hand to her, saying, "You're one hundred percent correct. He'd want you to chase your goals, whatever they might be."

"Those goals are not in Alaska, I know that much," she said. She held his hand, and he pulled her up with a reassuring grip.

Henry chuckled. "Well, let's get out of here then," he said, bending down to gather his pile of firewood. Olivia did the same, and the two headed back toward camp.

# 31

Olivia and Henry dropped off their first load of firewood on the woodpile at camp. Olivia noticed nothing new had been added and turned to Henry. "Looks like we're the first ones back," she said.

Henry saw the pile as well. "Yeah, it seems that way. I have a suspicion we're the only ones who make it back," he said. "I hope I'm just being paranoid, but that's just the way things seem to be going."

"Don't worry too much. Terry and Lee are probably working on breaking down a few larger branches. They didn't have a hatchet like us, after all."

Henry's tense expression softened as he considered her words. "You're right," he admitted. "I guess I'm just a bit on edge after everything that happened today."

"Same here," she mumbled as she organized the woodpile.

The two headed back toward the fallen log, loaded up with another armful of firewood, and then returned to camp. Upon their arrival, Olivia's optimism faded when she once again saw that no new wood had been added. Trying her best to hide the concern in her voice, she said, "I'm sure everything is fine. Let's not worry just yet. We still have one more load to bring in."

Henry nodded, but she could see the doubt in his eyes. It mirrored the uncertainty she felt. "You're right. They probably just got caught up in something and lost track of time."

Olivia tried to focus on the task at hand and pushed aside her growing anxiety. They quickly grabbed their last load of firewood and made their way back to camp as the daylight started to fade. As they arrived with their final load, there was still no sign of the others. The tension in the air was palpable, and Olivia exchanged a concerned look with Henry.

"Okay, now we worry," he said.

Taking a deep breath Olivia whispered, "Yes, yes, we do."

As long shadows crept through the forest before finally disappearing, Olivia and Henry headed toward the lake where Terry and Lee had gone. The rising moon provided a faint glimmer of light, enough to illuminate their immediate surroundings and the trail they traveled.

"Are we both assuming Owen is to blame here?" Olivia asked.

Henry crossed his arms and sighed. "I think we have to, but as terrible as it sounds, I'm hoping it's a rolled ankle or maybe a broken leg."

"If only."

As they continued forward, Olivia decided to call out for their missing companions. Her voice echoed through the darkness, "Lee! Terry! Where are you? You should be back by now. Terry! Lee!"

Henry chimed in, their voices resonating through the night, "Terry! Lee! Where are you?"

Amid the rustling of leaves, they heard a twig snap in the distance. A surge of hope and fear intertwined in her mind. Seconds later, another twig snapped.

"Terry! Lee! Is that you?" she called out, her voice quivering as she clutched her hatchet tightly.

There was no response. Another twig snapped, this time much closer. Her heart thundered in her chest and the blood drained from her face as she imagined what could be lurking in the shadows.

Another snap, even closer this time. She felt her pulse race, her senses on high alert. Any second now, she expected a figure to emerge from the shadows.

"This isn't funny. Where are you, guys?" Henry's voice echoed through the woods.

From a far-off distance, Lee's voice called out from behind them.

"Over here!" Olivia shouted back. Relief crashed over her when she realized the others were safe.

The snapping of twigs continued but now retreated into the shadows as Lee's voice grew closer. "Sorry, we're on our way back."

Remaining still, Olivia and Henry waited anxiously until Lee and Terry appeared from the darkness, their arms laden with sticks and logs.

"Sorry, we got turned around and couldn't find our way back. We heard you two shouting, and that got us back on track," Terry said.

Olivia was puzzled. She pointed toward the direction of the mysterious sounds. "You weren't just over there?"

"No," Terry said, equally perplexed by her question.

"Well, we're glad you're back now. But we just heard something coming toward us from that direction. I think it could have been Owen or maybe a bear. Whatever it was, you scared it off."

Terry considered her words and confidently replied, "Probably just a deer. Doubt a bear, and Owen is too much of a coward to ever show his face again."

Olivia's mind buzzed with conflicting thoughts, torn between the potential threats of both the bear and Owen. Her encounter with the bear earlier had been a chilling reminder of the dangers lurking in the wilderness, leaving her acutely aware of her vulnerability. But Owen's lingering presence also haunted her. She couldn't shake the unsettling feeling that he was still out there, hiding in the shadows and plotting his next move.

"I hope you had better luck on the resource-gathering mission than we did," Lee said.

"We did. I think we'll be fine for the night," Henry responded.

"Great, let's head back to camp then," Terry said, his tone dismissive.

# 32

"How should we all break out the night?" Henry asked as he settled into his place by the campfire.

"I was thinking about that. I don't think we have anything to worry about, to be honest," Terry said as he dropped his firewood on the pile.

Olivia glared at him. "We should still be prepared. I can take the first shift if that works."

"I'll take the second," Henry said.

"Third shift works for me," Lee added.

After a few moments of hesitation, Terry agreed to take the last shift.

As Olivia worked to get the fire pit lit, she said, "Hey everyone, let's make sure to stay vigilant tonight. If you see or hear anything unusual, wake the others immediately. And remember, the satellite phone is our lifeline out of here, so keep it safe."

"Please come get me if you need anything. Even if it's just to talk," Henry whispered to her.

She smiled warmly at him. "I appreciate that. Go rest up. It could be a long night."

"I hope not," he said as he retreated to his makeshift spruce needle bed.

Terry, who had been quietly listening, interjected, "Don't worry, the satellite phone is with me, and I'll make sure it stays safe."

While Terry and Lee settled down for the night, Olivia knelt by the fire pit. She couldn't shake the weight of the situation she had gotten into, especially how it affected her family. They were her rock when James died, and when she had the opportunity to return the favor by being there for them, she was stuck here, only making it worse for them.

She grabbed a few more sticks from the pile and set them beside the pit. Trying to distract herself from the overwhelming emotions, she focused on organizing the sticks into a neat structure, reminiscent of the log cabin method her father taught her to build during their camping trips. But that brought back more memories of her family, and her thoughts drifted to her parents sitting together, worried sick about their daughter's safety.

Her chest ached, imagining her mother and father's tearful conversations about her well-being. Her heart broke for them. She tried to regain control of her emotions by envisioning a brighter tomorrow—sitting on the plane, clutching the satellite phone in her hand, preparing to dial their number.

She played out the scene in her head. Her father answers, and she is so emotional she can barely speak. "Livvy, is that you?" he asks.

"Yes, Dad, it's me. I'm so sorry. I'm coming home."

Her father's voice breaks as he says, "Oh, Livvy, thank God. We've been so worried. Just come back to us."

Tears welled up in Olivia's eyes as she wished that scenario could be real at that very moment. But for now, all she could do was hope for a safe rescue and cling to the memory of her family's love and support.

She composed herself and wiped away the tears that streaked down her cheeks. Taking a deep breath, she refocused on the task before her. She added some kindling to the stick cabin she had prepared. Using one of the fireproof matches, she ignited the kindling, and the flames eagerly embraced the dry twigs, dancing to life.

Gradually, she added larger sticks from the pile, feeding the fire and nurturing its growth until it was substantial enough to support the weight of larger logs. With each addition, the flames leaped higher, casting a warm glow around the campsite. Satisfied with her work, she stepped back and found a comfortable spot to sit, observing the shadows of the flames dancing on the surrounding rocks. The crackling flames offered a sense of comfort, soothing her agitated spirit as she sought solace in their warmth.

She kept a watchful eye on the flames, occasionally adding a few more logs to keep the fire going. Yet, despite the comforting glow, uneasiness still lingered within.

Her mind raced at the thought of Owen lurking somewhere in the shadows. Every slight movement of a branch or rustle of leaves sent a jolt of fear through her veins, causing her senses to heighten, her fists to clench, and her teeth to grind. Together, she knew they were vigilant and prepared, but the fear refused to dissipate.

She jumped as a warm hand settled down on her shoulder. Her fingers instinctively reached for her hatchet, but when she realized it was Henry, she sighed with relief.

"Nice fire," he said as sat next to her.

"Thanks, I've had a bit of practice in my time. My dad taught me everything I know."

Henry's smile widened. "That's great. I bet you had a wonderful time learning all this stuff from him."

"I did. Why are you up? It's only been like twenty minutes."

He exhaled, his eyes reflecting the exhaustion of a day. "I couldn't sleep. Too many thoughts are running through my mind right now. I think I need to just sit and relax by the fire for a while."

"It is quite settling." She paused. "Henry, can I ask you something personal?"

"Of course."

"What was it like raising your son? Did you two ever go camping or do any outdoor activities together?"

Henry's face softened as he thought about his son. "Raising him was the best thing that's ever happened to me," he said warmly. "We went camping a lot when he was younger. It was one of my favorite things to do together. We'd explore the wilderness, fish, and enjoy each other's company. I miss those days."

"What happened?"

"Life happened. He grew up and became more interested in girls and sports. He then moved across the country for college. I told you he's expecting, right?"

Olivia nodded.

"Well, this whole experience has made me think. I want to move closer to him and be a part of that kid's day-to-day life. I've been thinking about that a lot since we've been out here. I want to hear the first word, see the first steps, all of it."

"I think that's a great idea. I've been thinking too. I'm done with Alaska. I'm going to grad school. I want more out of life than what the last few years have been."

Henry reached over, embracing her in a hug.

Olivia was startled once more by rustling outside the fire ring, and her surprise grew as Lee approached.

"Mind if I join you two?" he asked.

"Of course, have a seat," she said.

As he settled in, Henry asked him, "How are you holding up, Lee? You must be reaching your wit's end, I'd imagine."

"Close to it," Lee admitted. "It was a tough trip even before everything related to the plane crash happened."

"I heard you were trying to get a mine going. Is that true?" Olivia asked.

Lee shook his head. "Quite the opposite. I've been fighting against that mine for years. I work for an environmental group involved in a study on the mine's potential impact. It's dreadful to think about what will happen when it's built. I say *when*, not *if*, because I just found out it was approved. We'll certainly keep petitioning and doing everything we can to delay it, but it's inevitable."

"Oh my, that's awful. Is there anything I can do to help?" Olivia empathized.

"Maybe. We'll need all the help we can get to fight this thing. I'll let you know. If we ever get out of here, that is. Surprisingly, that's not what's bothering me the most though. My poor wife must be worried sick."

After a pause and a heavy sigh, he continued, "Several years ago, I was in South America conducting another mine study when a massive tropical storm moved in. It was the worst one I've ever seen. It wiped out our radio towers and destroyed our tents and vehicles. It took us a week to hike out and make contact. The first person I called was my wife. I'll never forget how terrified she was. It nearly broke her. I promised her I'd never put her through that again, and yet here we are. I feel so guilty," Lee confessed as his tears glistened and ran down his cheeks.

Olivia went over to him, offering a comforting hug that he readily accepted.

After some time, he stood up and said, "I'm sorry to bring you two down. I'm going to call it a night. Thanks for listening to me."

"You didn't bring us down at all. Thank you for sharing. Tomorrow, you'll see your wife, and it'll all be okay," Olivia said.

Lee nodded in acknowledgment before heading off to bed.

The two remained silent, watching the fire and taking turns adding more timber to the flames. As the fire crackled and danced, Olivia felt a sense of safety and comfort in Henry's presence. He turned to her and said, "You look tired. Please go get some rest."

She smiled back at him, appreciating his concern. "Thank you. I will. Please wake me up if you need anything," she added before settling down on her bed of spruce needles.

As she lay there, the sounds of nature began to soothe her nerves. She could hear an owl hooting in the distance, and another owl responding. As she listened to their conversation, she let out a deep sigh and drifted off to sleep.

# 33

"Olivia, wake up," Henry whispered.

Opening her eyes slowly, she propped up, trying to orient herself, only to realize no one else was around.

"Is it just you?" she asked.

Henry nodded.

"Where are the others?"

"I don't know, I just woke up. I went to bed after I woke up Lee for his shift."

"Great, just what we needed." Olivia tossed a small rock at the fire pit. As it struck, white smoke poured out of a black, charred log. The fire had been out for quite a while.

"Just when we thought things were heading in the right direction too. Where could they be?"

"I don't know, but I'm not happy about it."

Determined to do something productive, Olivia walked over to where they had hung the fish the night before, untied the knot, and slowly lowered the bag. Henry joined her, and once the bag was within reach, he reached inside and handed her one of the fish. "Well, this is nice," Henry remarked.

"Yes, it is," Olivia replied as she took a bite. "Hey, how many are left in there?"

"Oh, quite a few. It does look like some have gone missing since last night though. Do you think Owen raided it?"

"I doubt it. That would be pretty bold of him, wouldn't you think?" Olivia said as she took another bite of fish.

Henry shrugged his shoulders and chewed his food.

"Bold seems to be Owen's thing. Maybe it could have been him?" Olivia continued.

"I hate this. Where are Terry and Lee?"

"Do you think they would have gone to the lake early to fill up on water?"

"That's a thought. Want to hike out to see if they're there?"

Olivia hoisted the bear bag back up and tied it off. "Yeah, it sounds better than sitting here wondering and twiddling our thumbs."

As the two made their way toward the lake's clearing, Olivia made out the faint sound of voices in the distance. She picked up the pace, her walk transitioning into an all-out jog until she broke out onto the beach. She scanned left, then right. Nothing.

As she stood still, hoping to hear the voices again, Henry caught up to her.

"What's the matter?" he asked.

"Shh, I think I heard them."

The two paused, staying as silent as possible until she heard the voices again.

"There, to the left. Did you hear that?" she whispered.

"Yeah, I did."

"Should we head that way?"

Henry shrugged.

Before they could decide, two figures emerged from the trees and onto the beach several hundred yards away.

"Terry! Lee!" Olivia yelled.

In response, she heard yelling from the figures, but the words were indistinguishable.

"That has to be them. Let's go," she exclaimed, barely finishing her words before she sprinted toward them.

Henry ran alongside her as they closed the distance to the figures. "Where'd you both go?" Olivia asked as they all met up on the rocky shoreline.

"We called for help," Terry said bluntly.

"You did? Did you get a hold of someone? Are they on their way?" Henry blurted.

"Yeah, they're on their way," Terry added.

"Sorry we didn't wait for you. When Terry woke up for his shift, he grabbed the satellite phone and got ready to head out. He was going with or without me, and nothing I tried changed his mind," Lee said.

Terry shrugged, not seeming too concerned.

"You could have let us know," Olivia said.

"Thought you needed the sleep," Terry replied casually. "Anyway, help is on the way. Let's head back to camp, grab everything we have, and get back here. They're expecting a large signal fire. That's how they'll know exactly where we're at."

"Okay. Sounds good," Olivia said, her posture tensing and she made eye contact with Henry and then Lee.

As Terry marched down the shore to the trail, the three held back, out of his earshot.

"I'm so sorry. I don't know what's gotten into him. He woke up for his shift, looked at me, and then just flashed the phone in his hand before taking a few fish and walking off. He didn't even say a word. I couldn't let him go alone, so I rushed after him. He didn't say a single word the entire time, except for the phone call. I'm just as stunned as you are," Lee whispered.

"So strange. Thanks for keeping up with him. I'm just happy knowing help is on its way," Olivia said.

"Agreed," Henry added.

Lee nodded as the three made their way back toward camp.

# 34

The sound of rustling and rummaging caused Olivia's hair on the back of her neck to stand on end as she and the group approached camp.

Terry, sensing the tension, wasted no time as he rushed ahead. "Owen, is that you in our camp? It better not be."

"What if it is me?" Owen called back.

Olivia's hand instinctively went to the hatchet on her belt as she watched Terry's face harden. He turned to Olivia, and at that moment, she saw a side of him she hadn't seen before. His eyes narrowed, filled with a rage that made her uneasy, as he reached for her hatchet.

"Be careful. We're here to help too," she said, handing him the weapon.

"You all need to stay out of this. It's my business to handle, and I'll take care of it," Terry said as he marched forward.

Olivia exchanged a worried glance with Henry and Lee. They seemed just as unsure as she was about how to continue. She trusted Terry, kind of. But this anger was something she hadn't seen before, which left her feeling uneasy. He had also just taken quite the beating and was nowhere near recovered.

Terry stepped into the opening and stood face-to-face with Owen. Olivia could see a glint of fear in Owen's eyes, but his jaw was set defiantly, and that worried her.

"Last chance. Walk away or else," Terry warned.

Olivia had a sudden realization. When it was just the three of them, they managed to frighten Owen away. This time, they had Terry too. Surely, this would end the same way. She hoped he would come to this same conclusion too.

He didn't though. To her surprise, chaos erupted. Owen launched himself at Terry with startling speed. The force of his tackle knocked the hatchet out of Terry's hand, and they grappled for control, each trying to gain the upper hand.

Lee and Henry reacted, jumping in to help Terry, while Olivia froze, unsure what to do. Owen's aggression was evident as he kneed Lee in the stomach before punching Henry in the temple. Unexpectedly, she heard Terry scream in agony as he cried out, "He bit my finger!"

As Lee tackled Owen to the ground, Owen's eyes darted to the hatchet lying nearby. Despite Lee's weight pinning him down, Owen crawled towards the hatchet, reaching out for it. Olivia reacted swiftly, stomping on his hand with her boot. Owen's anguished cry filled the air, but she couldn't let him have the hatchet. She twisted her boot as it dug into his hand.

The others held him down as she secured the hatchet in her holster.

"Tie him up," she demanded.

"Give me your hands," Henry commanded Owen.

"Leave me alone!" Owen yelled back, still struggling against their grasp.

"Just do it," Terry growled, his voice firm as he kicked Owen in the ribs.

The force of the kick ended Owen's fight as he crumpled in pain. Olivia grabbed the paracord that had been used for Lee's restraints and handed it to Henry.

Olivia motioned for Terry to step away and whispered, "Take it easy. Go take a break and take care of your finger. We've got this under control."

Terry hesitated as he watched Owen but ultimately agreed and left the immediate surroundings, grasping his bloody finger.

Henry loosely tied Owen's hands while Lee watched closely. "No, not like that," Lee said, taking the paracord from Henry. "You need to tie it tight, or he'll escape. In Boy Scouts, I learned to tie a square knot. I'll show you how."

Lee tightly wrapped the paracord around Owen's hands in his lap, then proceeded to bind his ankles before connecting all four of his limbs, leaving Owen immobile.

"There, now he's not going anywhere," Lee said as he tested his knots.

Owen tested the bonds as well, frustration evident in his eyes, but Lee's knots held strong. Owen wasn't going anywhere, and he knew it. After he stopped struggling, he looked up at Olivia with a desperate expression. "Can I at least have some water?"

"Fine," she said as she tossed him a bottle.

"Real funny," Owen grumbled, gesturing to the restricting knots that bond his hands.

"You'll manage," she said.

Owen cast a pleading glance at both Lee and Henry, but they averted their eyes.

"Let's get to work collecting firewood by the beach. We need to signal for that rescue plane." Lee motioned for Olivia's hatchet, which she handed over without hesitation.

"I'll stay here with him," she said, locking eyes with Owen.

Lee turned to Henry, who agreed. "Sounds like a plan. I think Terry needs a second to deal with his finger."

Terry returned to camp and asked, "I need a moment with Owen. Olivia, step away for a couple of minutes. Also, leave that hatchet."

"Absolutely not," she said.

"I won't kill him," Terry retorted, fury still burning in his eyes.

Olivia stared at him. "You won't hurt him either," she said firmly, making her stance clear.

"Fine," he said reluctantly. "I need to go to the lake and wash the blood off my hand. Now would be a great time for a cigarette, too. I'm starting to go nuts."

"I can tell."

Terry snickered and followed the others out of the campsite toward the lake.

# 35

"So, about that drink?" Owen asked, gesturing with his chin to the water bottle.

"I said figure it out," Olivia replied. "You're the reason we're in this mess, so why should I help you?"

Owen's shoulders slumped as he tried to open the water bottle with his bound hands, but his efforts were futile. Frustrated, he rolled onto his back and managed to open it with a combination of both hands and his face. But when he tried to lift the bottle to his mouth, the majority of the water spilled out. Resigning to his fate, he glanced at Olivia.

"Why did you do it?" she asked as she studied Terry's blood smeared across his face. Lines of worry creased his forehead, and weariness weighed heavy in his eyes.

"You wouldn't understand."

"Try me," she pressed.

Owen hesitated before admitting, "Drugs."

"Drugs?"

Owen didn't respond immediately but instead shamefully looked down at the ground. "Terry had an amazing idea for a drug smuggling operation," he began. "We were supposed to be partners, splitting everything fifty-fifty. We would go on trips together, distributing drugs all over, but we never landed anywhere in Canada. We're not felons."

"I'm not sure that's how it works."

"Of course, it is," Owen insisted, his voice growing more animated. "That's what Terry told me, and that's the only reason I agreed to join him. I would never become a felon, no chance. Everything was going great. We were making so much money. I was able to put a flatscreen in every room of my trailer, even the bathroom." He paused and Olivia picked up a hint of pride in his voice.

"But then I found his secret stash," Owen continued, his anger returning. "He had stacks upon stacks of cash hidden in his closet. It must have been over a hundred thousand dollars. But I had only gotten about thirty thousand from him the whole time. He's a no good, rotten liar."

Olivia's emotions were in turmoil as she listened to Owen's account. She couldn't help but feel a sense of pity for the man, viewing him as a victim, persuaded into criminal activity by his mentor. She empathized with the desperation that had driven him to such extreme measures, but she also felt anger at the betrayal and the harm caused by his actions. She knew there was no justification for what he had done, even in the face of hardship.

Owen's tone turned flat, almost detached. "I may have made a mistake about the storm, but I saw it as my chance. So, I took his plane down. He thought it was turbulence, but I found a way to steer the plane without him knowing. It was easy. I knew we would survive the crash. Terry's an excellent pilot, but I took his plane from him. I figured I'd kill him after the crash, but he stashed that phone. I needed that phone first," Owen confessed. There was a forced determination in his words, as if he had reached a point of no return. Yet, underneath that facade, she detected a glimmer of vulnerability. He seemed to be grappling with the consequences of his actions.

"These are serious accusations. Do you have any evidence to back them up?" Olivia questioned.

"Yeah, I have a log of all our transactions and Terry's house is filled with drugs and cash. It's where we store everything."

She absorbed the weight of the revelation and struggled with conflicting emotions. On one side, she despised the man for purposefully stranding her, taking down the plane, and kidnapping Terry—being the reason for all the chaos. On the other hand, the mistreatment Owen endured tugged at her heart. Reflecting on the possible years of abuse Terry had subjected him to, she pitied the man.

"I hate to say this, but I believe you," she said. "We're getting out of here, and you'll have to pay for what you've done. Do you want to make sure Terry does too?"

Owen nodded his head.

"With your help, I'll make sure he does," Olivia said.

# 36

"Is everything okay?" Henry said as he entered camp alone.

"Fine. I did find out some interesting stuff. How about you? Where's Lee?" Olivia asked.

"He's with Terry. We gathered a lot of sticks, logs, and spruce needles and stacked them on the shore. They're working on starting a small fire so we can light the big one when we hear the plane coming. Ready to head to the lake?"

"Yeah, I'm ready to get out of here. But first, I need to tell you what Owen just told me." Olivia walked over to her belongings and shoved them into her pack.

"A desperate man will say anything to save himself," Henry whispered as he followed her.

"I know, but he says he has proof. It's why he took the plane down and why he kidnapped Terry. Aren't you at all curious?" she said.

Henry crossed his arms, contemplating. "Go on, you have my attention."

She explained to him what Owen had divulged about his involvement in drug running and how Terry had betrayed him, keeping the lion's share of the money. She revealed how he admitted to crashing the plane and how he planned on killing Terry.

Henry glanced over at Owen, who seemed to be lost in his thoughts, then turned back to Olivia. "What a mess. The two of them seemed a bit shady, but drug running? Attempted murder? What proof did he say he had?"

"A ledger, and a lot of cash and drugs at Terry's place," she said.

Henry approached Owen, with Olivia following closely as he knelt down to confront the captive.

"Is what you told her true? And you have a ledger to prove it?" Henry inquired.

"Every word of it. I don't know what a ledger is, but I wrote every trip down on my phone if that's what you mean. My phone's broken, but the cops should be able to get it," Owen replied. "Plus, there's tons of stuff at Terry's place right now. There's even stuff at the bottom of this lake."

Henry turned back to Olivia. "My brother's a cop. He'll take care of it."

She appreciated his help. Leaning closer, she whispered in his ear, "How do we manage Terry? I think he should probably go to jail too."

"I'll give my brother a call on the plane. I'll explain our whole situation minus the Terry details. We've hid things from our parents many times over the years and have a code phrase. We haven't used it for a long time, but he'll know something is up. He has a good buddy who's also a cop who lives somewhere around here. He'll have the right connections to make sure someone is there when we land," Henry said.

"Perfect." Olivia turned back to Owen. "It's all handled. Hand your phone to Henry, and Terry will be taken care of."

"Gladly, but I can't really move," Owen said, gesturing to his restraints. "It's in my front pocket though," he added.

Henry retrieved the phone from Owen's pocket, and the two began to untie the restraints, leaving his hands bound.

"Don't make any moves. It won't go well," Olivia warned as they finished untying the knots around Owen's legs.

Owen nodded, his demeanor more subdued than before. She noticed the shift in his body language, from defiance to resignation, as he accepted the gravity of his actions. It was unclear whether it was the weight of Terry's fate that brought about this change or if Owen had simply come to terms with the seriousness of the situation.

"Get up, we're getting out of here," Olivia commanded, urging Owen to his feet. Owen did as he was told, and the three of them set off toward the lake.

# 37

As they approached the shore, Olivia heard the distant yet familiar rumblings of a plane engine approaching.

"Hurry! Light the signal," she yelled.

"On it!" Lee responded, his eyes lit up with excitement as the sound of a plane roared in the distance.

He snatched a large branch covered with spruce needles and placed it on top of the small fire that was set up nearby. Within seconds, the needles erupted in flames.

Lee moved the burning branch to the top of a large pile of gathered sticks and logs. It was topped with even more spruce branches and the whole thing ignited into a magnificent inferno. Flames flickered and devoured the wood, and with it, billowing clouds of thick white smoke surged above the tree line.

Olivia watched in awe as the signal fire blazed brightly, its pillar of smoke stretching toward the sky. This was her lifeline, her beacon of hope guiding the rescuers to her location.

"Now *that's* a fire!" Lee yelled.

The sound of the approaching airplane intensified, sending a thrill of anticipation through Olivia. Her gaze remained fixed on the skies above the lake until, at last, she spotted it. "There it is—the plane! It's truly on its way," Olivia said.

"It looks like it spotted us too. It's circling back around to us," Henry said as he embraced Olivia and Lee in a group hug.

Olivia's attention was drawn to Owen as he attempted to attack Terry.

"You want another go?" Terry asked as he slammed him to the ground. He followed up with a stiff right hand to Owen's face, causing him to cower.

Olivia was about to intervene but was distracted when the aircraft made another pass around the lake, this time lower. It was a surreal moment, the realization that her rescue was imminent after enduring so much hardship.

"It's landing! It's really landing!" Henry announced.

Olivia could hardly believe it herself. Her emotions were overwhelming, and tears of happiness rolled down her cheek.

"Amazing," Lee cried out.

The plane made one last turn and then straightened out, rapidly descending in elevation. It seemed like it was going to crash into the water, but at the last moment, the nose of the plane tilted up and the plane's buoys gently kissed the lake's surface, creating graceful arcs. The wakes it generated rippled toward the shore.

As the plane slowly taxied to the shoreline, a commanding voice emerged, instructing them to stay put. The words brought a wave of reassurance and joy to the group, and they erupted into cheers.

Olivia's gaze shifted to her companions, and she saw a mixture of emotions mirrored in their faces: relief, joy, a sense of survival, and triumph. Except for Owen, who showed no interest in the plane at all and appeared defeated. His downcast eyes and distant expression spoke volumes. He appeared detached from the moment, burdened by the imminent future.

The plane stopped next to them by the shore, and a woman jumped out to greet them. She was short, a few inches over five feet, and she wore a black sweater with Medic written across the back. She called out in a friendly voice, "Hey! My name is Amy. I'm here to help get you all out of here."

Olivia was the first to reach Amy. "Thank you so much!" Olivia cried in relief. It was as if all the pent-up emotions of the harrowing journey were finding a release in the face of rescue.

Amy's smile was reassuring and her embrace warm when she held onto Olivia's hand and pulled her aboard. "Of course! Let's get you loaded!"

Once inside the plane, Olivia found a chair and stashed her pack at her feet. Her eyes followed the others as they boarded the plane. Henry and Lee guided Owen inside. He stumbled, his demeanor subdued and somber, and glanced at Olivia before taking the first seat near the door.

"Is there something I should know about?" Amy asked when she noticed the bindings on Owen's hands.

"It's a long story. One of us will explain in the air," Olivia said, fastening her seat belt.

Lee gave her a big high-five as he moved toward the back before he settled in a chair.

"We did it," Henry said, joining her on the plane.

"We sure did," she responded, her smile mirroring his.

Terry boarded the plane and settled into a seat next to the door after allowing Amy to clean and bandage his finger.

Amy closed the plane's door and sat next to the pilot. She scanned the group. "Everyone ready to go?"

Everyone except Owen shouted in unison, "Yes!"

Amy turned to Olivia and handed her a phone. "When we're in the air, feel free to make as many phone calls as you want. I'm sure your family is worried sick," Amy said.

Olivia leaned in close to Henry, handed him the phone, and whispered in his ear, "Call your wife first. Then, call your brother. Make sure he knows everything."

Henry thanked her and accepted the phone.

With everyone aboard and seated, the pilot's voice echoed through the cabin, "Alright, please fasten your seat belts and prepare for takeoff. It'll be bumpy getting out of here, but we should see smooth skies the rest of the way back."

"How long of a flight is it?" Olivia asked.

Amy gave her a reassuring smile and replied, "Not long. An hour, hour and a half, tops."

As the engine revved up, Olivia's gaze drifted to the window, watching the landscape outside. She admired the two massive peaks surrounding them one more time as the plane taxied across the lake. She marveled at the serenity of the place that had been their refuge, yet also their prison. Under different circumstances, it would have been difficult to leave such a captivating location. But not now; the time had come to leave. She was excited for her future. Excited to leave Alaska. Excited to move forward in her life.

As she relaxed in her seat, Olivia noticed Owen's eyes darting about. He seemed like a coiled spring, not the defeated man from before. She glanced at Terry's unbuckled seat belt. A sudden commotion seized her attention.

Owen had lunged for the door, desperately prying at it with his bound hands. The gut-churning urgency in his movements made Olivia's breath catch. "Owen, no!" she cried out in warning.

In an instant, the door swung open, and a rush of wind swept through the cabin.

Owen grabbed Terry by his shirt and catapulted them both out of the plane. Their bodies flailed through the air before vanishing into the water below.

Olivia turned back to her window but could only make out the water's wake from where they landed. Shock rooted her in place. The others seemed frozen by the surreal scene too.

Amy immediately shut the door and the pilot banked the plane around and began circling the lake, desperately searching for any sign of Owen and Terry. But the vast expanse of water revealed no traces. They were simply gone, swallowed by the cold depths.

"I'm so sorry," Amy said, her voice fracturing the silence. "We'll send help but for now…"

Her words faded to background noise as reality crashed down on Olivia. Tears blurred her vision. She should have done something—anything—to prevent this. Exhaustion and grief pressed down as she replayed those last terrifying seconds.

Beside her, Henry squeezed her hand, a lifeline of support amid the roiling emotions.

Neither of them had cared much for Owen, considering it was his fault they were in this predicament. Yet, deep down, she knew he didn't deserve to go this way.

Then there was Terry. A hard man who had pushed his friend to the breaking point. He didn't deserve this either. They both deserved a jail cell, not being lost to the wild.

As the plane reached cruising altitude, Henry handed her the phone. "Call your family. They're worried sick about you."

Olivia took the phone and dialed her father's number, her anticipation building. She pressed the call button and brought the phone to her ear. As it started to ring, a surge of emotions overwhelmed her and tears streamed down her face.

Her father's voice finally came through, and she choked back her sobbing as she managed to say, "Dad."

"Livvy, is that you?"

With a quivering voice, she responded, "Yes, Dad, it's me. I'm so sorry. I'm coming home."

# 38

Two months had passed since being rescued. Olivia was driving home from a graduate program interview. As she tapped her foot on the break for a slow truck ahead, her phone rang. A grin crept across her face when she recognized Henry's name on the caller ID. She set her floral mug down in a cup holder before answering.

"Henry! How are you?"

"Great to hear your voice. I'm doing well. My wife and I are in California right now, and we just put an offer on a house in the same neighborhood as my son. Fingers crossed."

"Oh, that's amazing! I'm so thrilled for you. I hope everything works out."

"Did I tell you about the other good news?" Henry asked.

"Better than a move out west? Tell me."

"They just told us they're having a boy! I'm so excited."

"That's incredible news! I'm so happy for you. You'll have to take him out here so I can teach him how to fish," Olivia said, barely containing a smile.

"Of course, he'll only learn from the best. By the way, how did your interview go? It was today, right?"

"Yes, it was. Good memory. I'm driving home from it right now. And you were right, she remembered you. Expect her to reach out anytime. I have a feeling she'll call you as a reference."

"Anything for you."

"Everything went well though. This program sounds fantastic, and I'm excited about it," Olivia said. "If I get in, I'm positive it's the one for me."

You're a shoo-in, Olivia." Henry paused momentarily before continuing, "Hey, did you hear from Lee today?"

"I didn't. What's up?"

"The lake finally froze over last week." Henry paused once more, seeming to struggle to continue. "It seems that marks the end of the search for Terry and Owen."

"Wow, I can't believe it. They never found any sign of them, huh? Do you think one of them made it out?"

"Who knows, but if anyone could, it would be Terry."

"Very true."

"Oh! Looks like she's calling me now to check your references. I'll make sure to put in a good word for you. Talk to you later!"

"Thanks, Henry. Best of luck with the house!"

After hanging up, Olivia drove on in contemplative silence. She exited the interstate and headed toward the familiar gravel road that led her home. As memories of Owen and Terry lingered, she wiped away a final tear. Though lasting trauma would remain from her ordeal, she was determined to move forward. She picked up the floral mug and took one last sip. A new life awaited, full of hope.

From the Author

Thank you for embarking on the journey of *Betrayed in the Wild.* Crafting these characters and this story has been a labor of love, and I am extremely grateful that you have joined me on this adventure.

As an independent author, reader reviews and book recommendations play a vital role in helping others discover my work. If you enjoyed this novel, I would appreciate your leaving a review on Amazon or Goodreads.

Additionally, if you could recommend this book to your friends, family, or social media, your support would be amazing. If you'd like to keep up with Olivia and her next adventure, please visit my website: Ryan-Cuddy.com.

Thanks,
Ryan Cuddy